Fervent Surrender: An Age Gap BDSM Erotic Romance

Surrender To Love, Volume 3

Leah Addison and Willow Watkins

Published by Leah Addison, 2024.

Copyright 2024 by Leah Addison & Willow Watkins
All rights reserved. No part of this publication may be reproduced, stored or transmitted in any form or by any means, electronic, mechanical, photocopying, recording, scanning or otherwise without written permission from the author. It is illegal to copy this book, post it to a website, or distribute it by any other means without permission.
This novel is entirely a work of fiction. The names, characters and incidents portrayed in it are the work of the authors imagination. Any resemblance to actual persons, living or dead, events or localities is entirely coincidental.
The characters depicted in this work of fiction are 18 years of age or older.

Table of Contents

Chapter One 1
Chapter Two 7
Chapter Three 14
Chapter Four 21
Chapter Five 29
Chapter Six 34
Chapter Seven 40
Chapter Eight 46
Chapter Nine 54
Chapter Ten 60
Chapter Eleven 66
Chapter Twelve 71
Chapter Thirteen 76
Chapter Fourteen 81
Chapter Fifteen 86
Epilogue 91

Chapter One

Alex:

I sit at a table at Surrender, the BDSM club that I co-own with three of my closest friends. Each of them has a beautiful young woman either on their lap or kneeling at their feet as they occupy the other chairs around the table. They are all laughing and chatting together, but I hardly hear them as I get lost in my own thoughts.

Some people might describe the almost painful pang in my chest as jealousy, as I watch my closest friends in the world show affection to the women in their lives. But I prefer to call it curiosity.

Sure. That word works just as well as any.

I'm not sure I've ever seen what a happy relationship looks like before now. All I can remember from my childhood is my mom and dad screaming at each other almost constantly. And then even that unhappy family had fallen apart when Mom had caught Dad cheating with multiple other women.

So I've never let a woman get close enough to find out if relationships really are as painful as they had seemed when I was growing up. All I allow myself is one night here or there with some beautiful woman, and then I'm gone.

Catching feelings for someone is the last thing I want. I just want to be able to take control of someone for a night, and enjoy the sounds of her moaning my name while I make her come until she almost passes out. Then after that, it's over. That's always been enough for me.

But now, I'm forty-six, and just starting to think that maybe this love thing doesn't look so bad after all.

"Why the long face, Alex?" someone asks, pulling me out of my thoughts.

I blink and bring my attention back to the table to find all three of my friends and their women staring at me. I've got no idea who it was that spoke, so I shrug my shoulders.

"I'm fine," I say, glancing over at the people on the dance floor just so I don't have to look anybody in the eye.

"Ahhh, it seems he's looking for his next willing victim," Grace says with a giggle, from her safe spot on Oliver's lap.

I laugh and roll my eyes. "Not at all," I say. And it's true. The last thing I'm in the mood for tonight is a random hook-up, although usually, that would be my go-to fix in the past whenever I felt like this. But it just doesn't seem to help anymore, so it's losing its appeal.

"Are you sure?" Elijah asks. He points over to a young woman who is standing alone at the edge of the dance floor, looking around awkwardly. "It looks like she's new, so she probably hasn't heard about your reputation as a ladies' man. You might be in with a shot, Alex."

I flip him the bird before turning my attention back to the woman. It's true that she's fucking breath-taking, with her long dark hair cascading down her back, and her curves that look like they were made for a very lucky man to explore. The pink floaty dress she's wearing looks out of place here, with the couples either in fetish gear, or the men in suits while their submissives remain naked. But it looks so damn cute on her that she manages to pull it off.

Any other night, and I might have given it a shot. But with the mood I'm in right now, I'm not sure I want to put her through the torture that my company would probably be.

I lift my eyes to her face and realize she seems vaguely familiar. Have I slept with her before? That would definitely be a possibility. I've probably fucked half the women in this room. But I'm pretty sure that, if I had slept with this beauty before, I would have remembered it.

As I watch, a man approaches her. A smile breaks out across the woman's face, but it seems like more of a polite gesture as she takes a step back to put some space between her and the other man.

"Oh, shit," I mutter, as it suddenly hits me where I know her from. I can't believe it took me so long to figure it out, but then she's the last person I would expect to see in a place like this.

I rise from my chair. "I'll be back soon," I say to my friends, before I begin striding over to her.

"Look, it's just one drink," I hear the guy say to her as I approach him from behind. "What harm will it do? I can even take you on a tour of the club if you like. Are you a first-time submissive?"

I place my hand on his shoulder and grip tightly as I turn him around to face me. I let out a sigh. Why the fuck is Adam creeping around the new girl? We have strict rules at the club that have been put in place to protect the submissives from the hoards of predatory Doms that seem to exist these days. Especially the new ones like Ellie, who don't have the experience to tell the good Dominants from the bad. Adam has always seemed like one of the good guys, but I might have to keep a closer eye on him in the future.

"She's here as my guest," I say, my voice firm.

As one of the owners of the club, my word is final, so I know he won't try to fight me for her. But judging by the way his fists flex at his sides, he looks tempted to give it a try.

It surprises me to realize I'd be willing to fight him too, if it came to that. A strange possessive feeling washes over me at the thought of sweet Ellie being taken advantage of by anyone. Or just being approached by any man who isn't me.

But now isn't the time for thoughts like that, and I tuck it away in my pocket so I can re-examine it later when I'm alone.

"Fine," he mutters, before turning away from me, and I release my grip on his shoulder. "It was a pleasure to meet you, Ellie," he says, flashing the woman a smile. "I hope we can catch up later."

"Maybe," she says, giving him another one of those polite smiles, even though her body language screams her discomfort.

As soon as Adam is gone, she relaxes, and a genuine smile spreads across her lips that brightens up her entire face.

"Hi, Alex," she says.

I stare at her, dumb-founded. Ellie seems completely out of place at a club like this. A club dedicated to the more deviant side of life.

She's young, probably in her early twenties, and she's my new neighbor at the place I moved into just a couple of months ago. She lives there with her mom, although I never see the older woman about much. I do hear her screaming a lot, though. From the slurred and often incoherent shouting, my guess is that Ellie's mom likes to drink, but I've never met her, so it's hard to say what her problem is.

Ellie seems sweet enough, though. Sometimes I run into her in the morning, when I'm heading to my office at the law firm I set up a few years ago, and she's heading to her job at the library. I often wonder if she's the target of her mom's temper tantrums. Perhaps it's no wonder I feel a little protective of her, knowing that she's probably going through some stuff at home.

Honestly, I've always thought she was pretty, but I've never thought of making a move. I don't shit on my own doorstep, and it would be a little difficult to walk away after one night if I only live next door. But, seeing her tonight with her hair and make-up done nicely, and without the thick-rimmed glasses she usually wears, I can see she's a hell of a lot more than just pretty.

She's a tempting little morsel who suddenly seems a lot more difficult to resist. Especially when she is standing in the middle of a BDSM club. Could she be a submissive? She's always seemed too innocent for that.

Perhaps she's here looking for someone to corrupt her.

I quickly shake that thought out of my head and place a gentle hand on her forearm.

"What are you doing here, Ellie?" I ask.

"I came here looking for you, Alex," she says, smiling up at me.

I have to hold back a groan. Jesus Christ. What is she playing at? My dick is standing to attention, and all too eager to play along with whatever game she has in mind. The greedy little fucker.

"Come on, I'll get you a drink, and then you can tell me what's going on," I say, leading her over to a quiet booth at the back of the club.

I know my friends are all staring at me, probably wondering what's going on. No doubt they think I'm making a move on her, even though that couldn't be further from the truth - no matter how tempted I might be.

I'm just trying to keep her safe.

And trying to figure out what she's doing here.

As soon as we're seated, I signal to the waitress and order a couple of soft drinks for us. I don't think alcohol is a good idea right now. I need to keep my head clear so I don't end up doing anything stupid, and it's a good idea if Ellie does the same.

Once the waitress has gone to fetch our drinks, I lean forward, placing my elbows on the table between us as I focus all my attention on the beautiful young woman in front of me.

"So what's going on, Ellie? Why are you here to see me?"

Her face flushes a deep shade of red, and her bottom lip disappears between her teeth. It makes her look even sexier.

"Ummm..."

She trails off and stares down at her hands, which are clasped together on the table top.

"Well, a while ago, you told me that you owned this place, and I got curious because I didn't know much about kinky things. But I started doing some research and now I'm... curious."

The way she stumbles over the word curious, and the way her cheeks redden even further, makes me think she means something a little more than she's letting on.

I can remember mentioning the club and the fact that I'm a co-owner in passing during one of our early morning interludes out on the front lawn as I'd been leaving for work. And honestly, I'd only said it because I thought it would be amusing to get my innocent neighbor feeling flustered. To shock her a little.

But it seems now I'm the one left feeling those things.

"So that's why you're here? To do some experimenting and learn more about the lifestyle?"

I try to keep my voice steady, ignoring the way my dick is throbbing uncomfortably against the zipper on my pants. Images of her tied down and screaming my name are already rushing through my head, sending even more blood down to my groin.

"Kind of," she says, squirming in her chair a little before lifting her eyes to meet my gaze. "I was hoping that you might be able to teach me, Alex."

I stare at her, open-mouthed. Jesus Christ. I never would have believed my pretty and shy neighbor was kinky at all, and I sure as hell didn't think she had it in her to chase me down at a BDSM club and ask me to teach her about dominance and submission.

Yet here she is, surprising the fuck out of me.

And damn, now I'm even more intrigued about her, which is dangerous territory for me.

I haven't got a clue what to say to her, but luckily for me, the waitress returns with our drinks, giving me a moment to gather my thoughts.

It's not often that I'm caught off-guard or left speechless, but damn if Ellie hasn't managed that effortlessly tonight.

I'm almost tempted to take her up on her offer.

Almost.

Chapter Two

Ellie:

The way Alex looks at me across the table as the waitress hands us our drinks has my heart pounding harder than ever. I wish I could read him, but he seems completely unfazed by my request.

Does that mean he gets women asking him to dominate them all the time?

I push aside that thought, as well as the envy that rises up inside me. It's none of my business what he does.

But after spending the last few months lost in daydreams about the sexy older man next door, it's difficult not to be upset about him being with other women.

The waitress disappears, and I can't help but notice the longing looks she throws at Alex. But he doesn't see them. Not when he's staring at me so intently. It feels like he's trying to read every last little thought in my mind, and I hope he can't, given that most of them include him doing very lewd things to me.

"So, I assume you want me to answer questions you have about dominance and submission?" he asks, one eyebrow raising slightly.

I feel the heat flooding my face. "Ummm, well... if that's how you would prefer to teach me..." I say, my words and my earlier confidence suddenly leaving me completely.

Alex leans forward across the table, bringing his face closer to mine. "Tell me how you want me to teach you, then, Ellie."

There is no hint of a request in his words. Ever since the time he mentioned he owned a BDSM club with his friends, I've had trouble reconciling the cheerful and laid back man next door with the kind of Doms I was coming across in my research. Research that mostly consisted of reading dirty books and watching adult movies.

But I can see it now. While there is still the warm kindness I'm used to seeing in his green eyes, there is now a steely set to his jaw, and a firmness to his tone that sends shivers down my spine.

I like this side of Alex.

A lot.

The arched brow lifts a little higher, and I begin squirming in my seat. He expects an answer, and the way he's looking at me makes my brain feel fuzzy, making it hard to disobey.

"I was hoping you would show me in a more personal way... Sir."

I hesitate before adding that final word, unsure if it's the right thing to do. But as soon as I say it, Alex's gaze seems to soften, and his lips curl up into a slight smile.

"Have you ever submitted to anybody before, Ellie?" he asks, tilting his head to the side as he looks at me.

"No, Sir," I whisper.

I don't mention that I don't have any experience with men whatsoever, besides one kiss with a boy in my first year of college. My mom has done her best over the years to warn me off men altogether, telling me they are all disgusting pigs, and they all cheat. And whenever I've mentioned having a crush, she's always made it clear that I'm not allowed to date, often getting mad and screaming at me. Not that she needs much of an excuse to do that. Especially after she's had a drink.

If Mom gets her way, I'll be single and still living with her until old age.

The only reason I'm here tonight is because I told my mom that I'm staying over with a friend. A friend who knows she's acting as an alibi for me, and who's ready to lie to my mom if she calls.

It's pathetic that I'm having to sneak around and lie like this when I'm twenty-three, but it's safe to say my mom's got issues.

Alex nods briefly, as if I've just given him the answer he was expecting; then he looks out over the crowd of people on the dance floor, chewing on his lower lip.

I take a moment to appreciate just how good he looks close up. With his dark hair, a slight hint of stubble covering his jaw, and his green eyes, he's gorgeous. Even though he hasn't agreed to anything yet, my mind is already racing, imagining all the things he could do to me.

Oh god, what if he says no? I'll be so damn embarrassed. It took all the courage I had to come and talk to him tonight, and I only did it because I really was spending a stupid amount of time thinking about him. Alex has almost become an obsession, and I knew I wouldn't be able to stop fantasizing about him until I at least asked him.

My palms feel clammy, and a lump rises up in my throat as I wonder if perhaps he's going to reject me. I don't even know if I can stand the humiliation if that happens.

I should have kept my mouth shut. I'm not even a part of this world.

"Let's go somewhere we can talk about this properly," he says, rising from his chair and holding out his hand.

I let out a breath and smile, relieved that he doesn't seem ready to throw me out of the club just yet.

Taking his hand, I let him lead me through the club, past the dance floor, and down a dimly lit hallway. The music begins to fade, and all I can hear are the sounds of the moans and screams coming from the play rooms, as well as a couple of loud slaps.

My pulse races, and I find myself becoming a little nervous. Alex squeezes my hand gently, and the contact is reassuring. I can't believe I'm doing this.

He comes to a stop outside a room and pushes the door open, gesturing for me to go inside.

I take a few small steps, then stop, my eyes going wide as I take in the contents of the room. There is a large bed in the center, covered in black satin sheets, and there are hooks on all four walls, holding all kinds of things I can barely even name. There are different kinds of restraints, including leather cuffs, rope, and even metal handcuffs. As well as various spanking implements. There is a mahogany dresser along one wall that holds several dildos and butt plugs of various different sizes.

As I begin walking slowly around the room, staring in wonder at all the objects, my stomach flip-flops, and I begin to question what I'm doing.

How can I possibly hope to satisfy a man who uses all these things?

Alex closes the door, and I can hear the lock click into place behind me.

"Are you sure you want me to show you how it feels to submit?" he asks, and I turn to look at him.

He's still standing by the door, with his arms folded across his chest in a way that makes his biceps bulge, and his gaze is fixed on me.

"Yes, Sir," I say, my voice a little shaky, but there is no doubt in my mind.

He nods. "There will be some ground rules," he says, his voice still holding that firm tone that makes my knees feel weak.

Euphoria rises up inside me. He isn't going to turn me away.

"Anything you want, Sir," I reply, my voice sounding breathless.

"First of all, this is a one-night thing, Ellie. I'm not looking for a relationship right now, and I can't offer you anything more than just tonight."

The excitement I had been feeling a few moments earlier deflates a little, but I nod in agreement with that rule. At least I get to have one night with Alex. And I already know it's going to be the best night of my life so far. I'm just grateful he isn't pushing me away.

Besides, I don't think I'd be able to hide an actual relationship from my mom and her prying eyes, so this is probably for the best, anyway.

"Two, we won't be having sex. I am perfectly capable of dominating you and making you scream with pleasure without my dick even coming out of my pants."

10

Now there is a heavy dose of arousal mixing with the disappointment I feel. His confidence, and his dirty words, are a complete turn on, and my panties are growing damp already. I have no doubt that he's more than capable of following through on his promise. While I might have come here wishing that Alex would take my virginity, I'm smart enough to realize this is a once in a lifetime opportunity for me.

"Three, even though I will be in control, you will have the power to stop things at any time. All you have to do is say your safe word. Do you know what a safe word is, Ellie?"

I nod quickly. "Yes, Sir."

"Good girl. And what would you like your safe word to be?"

The praise makes me tingle with delight, and I have to force myself to focus on his question.

"Ummm, can it be peaches, please, Sir?"

Alex laughs, and the sound makes me smile.

"Peaches, it is," he says as he walks towards me, stopping right in front of me. He grips my chin and tilts my head up until I'm looking into his eyes.

A whimper escapes me. He's so close that I can smell the intoxicating mix of his cologne and the scent of pure maleness that's all his own. My heart is hammering so hard, I'm certain he can hear it.

His pupils dilate, and I see the corner of his lips twitch.

"Now, what I want you to do is go and pick three of the items in the room that you are most curious about, and then bring them to me."

He releases his grip on my chin and takes a step back, and I miss the warmth emanating from his body almost immediately.

I hesitate, unsure where to start. The room is filled with so many things that I've only seen online, and it's a little overwhelming.

I swallow nervously and begin looking around the room. My gaze stops on the metal cuffs hanging from the wall. I walk towards them, reaching up to touch the cold metal, but I'm not sure they are right for me.

Instead, I continue wandering around the room, finally finding a long length of red silk. My fingers tease across the fabric, and I'm instantly curious what Alex would do with it. I pick it up, holding it in my hand as I continue inspecting the other items.

It feels like it takes forever, because it's hard to choose only three things when, in reality, I want to try them all. But I pick up a blindfold and a set of nipple clamps attached by a thin silver chain. I'm not sure why, but as soon as I lay my eyes on them, I feel a flutter of excitement between my thighs.

I walk back to Alex and hold out my three choices in hands that are trembling slightly. His eyes roam over them, as if assessing my decision carefully.

One corner of his lip curls up into a smirk that makes my heart skip a beat.

"Good girl, Ellie. I think these are going to do very nicely," he murmurs, his eyes meeting mine.

I'm transfixed by the look of raw desire in them, and it has heat flooding through my body.

"I have to say, I'm not at all surprised about the red silk and the blindfold. They are choices that fit well with what I know about you already. I can imagine you are the type of young woman who is curious about the more sensual side of BDSM. But the nipple clamps; they do surprise me a little. I think you're also curious about what it would be like to feel a bit of pain with your pleasure."

He doesn't phrase it as a question, so I don't respond. But I'm sure the rush of color to my face is enough of an answer for him.

"I'm going to have fun with you tonight, Ellie," he says, his soft, plump lips turning up into a full grin now. "Are you ready to begin?"

"Yes, Sir," I reply, without hesitation.

I am more than ready for him.

I have been since the moment I first met him.

Chapter Three

Ellie:

"Take off your clothes," he commands, and there is no hint of uncertainty or nervousness left in my body.

I obey him immediately, eager to do whatever it takes to make him happy. I need to know what it feels like to be dominated, to be controlled. To submit to the one man who has captured my attention like no other.

My fingers shake a little as I remove my dress, dropping it onto the floor next to me. When I'm down to just my underwear, I hesitate, but I can feel Alex's eyes on me, watching every move, and so I continue, letting the last pieces of fabric fall away.

Once I'm completely naked, I look up and meet his gaze. My cheeks flush with embarrassment.

"You are a beautiful woman, Ellie," he says, the corners of his mouth turning up in a small smile.

My face grows hotter, but a small rush of excitement flows through me.

"Thank you, Sir."

His smile grows wider. "Good girl."

Alex places the blindfold and the nipple clamps on the edge of the bed and approaches me, carrying only the red strip of silk. He moves behind me, and he's so close that his warm breath brushes over the back of my neck. It sends a shiver down my spine.

"Do you remember your safeword, pet?" he asks in a softer tone, even as his fingers wrap around my slender wrists to pull them gently behind my back.

"It's peaches, Sir," I tell him, my breath catching in my throat as I feel him begin wrapping the silk around my wrists, bringing it between them and around to bind them together at the small of my back.

"Good girl. And you must use it if you need to. If I do something you don't like, or it gets too much, just say it and I will stop straight away. Submission isn't about having someone do things to you that you don't want. It's about letting someone you trust give you everything you could ever want and need - even when you don't know it's what you want yet."

His voice is deep and gruff, his lips brushing against my ear as he speaks. It's making me feel things I never knew I could feel, and the heat between my thighs is spreading.

Once he has tied my hands securely, he walks around to my front and looks down at me. I'm completely naked, while he's still wearing the tight black t-shirt and black pants that cling to his body. Everything about him is just so damn masculine. It's enough to send a quiver through my body.

"I promise I'll use my safeword if I need to, Sir," I say, the words coming out on a whimper.

He grins at me and nods. "Good, because I can't wait to start playing with your body and hearing you moan for me."

Before I can respond, Alex scoops me up in his arms and settles with me on the bed, with him sitting back against the headboard and me sitting between his thighs, my back against his chest. He reaches over and grabs the blindfold and nipple clamps, drawing them closer.

A soft moan of anticipation escapes me as I realize he will be using them on me soon. He'll be touching me when I'm bound and blindfolded, helpless and at his mercy.

Just the thought of it makes me embarrassingly wet, and I squirm a little between his muscular thighs.

He chuckles softly and slips the blindfold over my eyes. It's soft and silky, and blocks out all the light, plunging me into darkness.

"How does that feel, pet?" he asks, his breath warm against my cheek.

Knowing he's so close that I can feel him surrounding me with his strength and control is an intoxicating feeling. I relax back against him, leaning my head back on his shoulder while my bound hands remain trapped between our bodies.

"It feels good, Sir."

"Good," he replies, and I feel him reach around me and cup one of my breasts.

My breath catches in my throat as he teases my nipple between his thumb and forefinger, rolling it until it's a stiff peak, and I can't help but arch my back, pressing myself more firmly against his hand.

Alex laughs again, a low, throaty chuckle that fills my body with a warm glow. "You like it when I touch you, pet?"

"Yes, Sir," I breathe, a shudder running through my entire body as he gives my nipple a sharp pinch, sending a jolt of pleasure-pain straight to my pussy.

I'm dripping wet already, and I can feel my arousal coating my inner thighs. I want to touch myself so badly, but the silky restraints around my wrists make that impossible.

He brings his hand to my other breast, teasing both nipples at the same time until I'm squirming shamelessly. Each little touch sends tingles to my clit, making me feel like I could come from being touched like this alone.

"Please, Sir," I whimper.

His lips brush against the side of my neck, a feather-light kiss that makes goosebumps rise on my skin. "What do you need, Ellie?"

"I... I don't know," I admit, my voice barely more than a whisper. I've never felt so completely lost to sensation.

"Do you need me to take care of you? To make you feel good, pet?"

"Yes, Sir," I moan, writhing against him. "Please."

"Alright, pet, I'll take care of you," he murmurs, kissing his way along my neck, his stubble scratching against my delicate skin.

His hands continue to play with my nipples, teasing them into stiff peaks. He pinches them gently, and it sends another jolt of pleasure straight to my clit. It feels incredible.

My breath comes in shallow gasps, and I'm so turned on that I'm practically vibrating with need.

My brain is so fuzzy now that it takes me a second to realize he's pulled his hands away from my breasts, and then another second to register the sensation of something cold and solid pinching at my nipples.

"Ooh," I whimper, as the metal clamps pinch the sensitive little buds tightly.

They feel heavy and foreign, and the sensation is strange, but not entirely unpleasant.

"How does that feel, pet?" Alex asks, his breath hot against my ear.

"It feels... good, Sir," I whisper, unable to find any other words.

He chuckles softly, then a sharp pain shoots through my nipples as the clamps pull at the stiff peaks, tugging them outwards from my body.

Alex must be pulling on the chain, toying with me as I remain helpless.

A loud moan escapes me, and my hips buck instinctively. The pressure of the clamps is intense, but it's the kind of pain that just adds to the pleasure building inside me.

"Do you want me to make you come, pet?" Alex asks, and the desire in his voice is unmistakable.

"Yes, please, Sir," I beg.

I feel his hand slip between my thighs, and I spread my legs shamelessly for him, wanting nothing more than to feel his touch on my most intimate parts.

His fingers trace a line up my inner thigh, teasing and torturing me. The ache inside me grows, and I bite my lower lip to keep from begging again.

It's such a helpless feeling, having the sensations keep building inside me until I feel like I might go crazy, but being unable to give myself any relief. But this is what I came here for. To find out what true surrender really feels like. And Alex is giving me exactly what I need.

Finally, after what feels like an eternity, his fingers graze my slick folds, and another moan escapes me.

"You're so wet for me, pet," he murmurs, his fingers exploring me with maddening slowness.

"Yes, Sir. Please, please touch me."

He presses two fingers inside me, filling me completely. The sensation is so intense that I can't help but cry out. He thrusts in and out of me slowly, his palm pressing against my clit with each movement.

The pleasure builds inside me, and I feel myself spiraling towards the edge. My body is on fire, and the tension is coiling inside me, ready to snap.

A sharp sensation adds to everything else I'm feeling as Alex begins tugging on the chain between the clamps again, making my head spin with the intense mix of pleasure and pain.

"Oh god, Sir," I gasp, my whole body trembling as I near the edge.

"Don't you dare come without permission, Ellie," he growls in my ear, even as his fingers begin pumping faster in and out of me. "You're my pretty little toy to play with tonight, and I'm not ready to put you out of your misery yet."

I moan, a desperate, needy sound that comes from somewhere deep inside me. I'm so close, and with each thrust of his fingers, I feel myself teetering on the edge, the tension growing tighter and tighter.

"Please, Sir, I need to come," I whimper, barely able to think straight. "I don't think I can stop it. Please, Sir."

"Oh, you'll stop it, or I'll have to punish you," he says, his voice a low rumble in my ear. "You don't want to find out what happens to bad girls who disobey, do you, Ellie?"

"No, Sir, please," I gasp, my body taut as a bowstring.

I'm so close that it's taking every little bit of willpower I possess to hold back. Every part of me is aching for release.

"Please what, pet?" he murmurs, his lips brushing against the shell of my ear. "You want me to make you come all over my fingers? Make you scream my name as you writhe in ecstasy?"

"Yes!" I gasp, the word coming out almost like a sob as the desperation takes hold.

"Then do it," he growls, the words low and commanding. "Come for me, Ellie."

His fingers thrust hard and fast, and at the same time, a deep and painful ache appears in my nipples as the metal clamps that had been pinching them are released.

The combination of sensations, along with Alex's command to come, is enough to push me over the edge. I let go, crying out as the orgasm crashes through me, the waves of pleasure overwhelming me.

"Oh, Sir," I moan, my body convulsing as he continues to pump his fingers in and out, drawing out every last ounce of pleasure from me.

It's the most intense thing I've ever felt, and I'm lost in the haze of ecstasy.

When the orgasm finally subsides, I slump back against Alex, utterly spent and completely sated. He slips his hand between our bodies to untie the silk around my wrists, then he pulls off the blindfold. Not that it matters. I'm too exhausted to move or open my eyes, anyway.

His strong arms envelope me, holding me against the broad and solid expanse of his chest.

"You were such a good girl, Ellie," he murmurs softly in my ear. "You made me so proud."

A sleepy smile tugs at the corners of my lips, while a warm feeling fills my chest.

Despite what Alex said at the start, I don't want this to be a one-off. I want another chance to be a good girl. To make him proud.

I'm willing to do anything it takes to be with him again.

Because I've just had a taste, and now I'm certain that no one else will ever make me feel this way again.

"Thank you, Sir," I whisper.

Alex kisses the top of my head and runs his fingers through my hair in a soothing motion that soon has my heavy eyelids drooping even more.

I'm safe with him. And because of that, I'd give him the entire world if I could.

But all I have to offer him is my submission.

I just have to hope it's enough to make him change his mind about a relationship.

Chapter Four

Alex:

What the hell had I been thinking?

I took things too far with Ellie last night at the club. And now, all I've been able to think about at work today is the sound of her moans, and how much I loved the breathy sound of her voice as she'd begged me to let her come.

I let out a sigh as I pull into the street where I live. All day I've been in the worst fucking mood, mad at myself for taking a taste of a sweet treat that I know I'll just keep craving. But now I'm almost home, I plan to lock that front door, and jerk off to oblivion in the hope of working Ellie out of my system. Then I'm going to hide from my issues in the blissful numbness of sleep. I hope.

It sounds like the perfect way to spend the evening.

But as I pull up onto my driveway, I fear fate has other plans for me.

Ellie is sitting out on the front porch of their house, shivering slightly in the cool early evening air as she keeps her arms wrapped around herself. She's still wearing her work clothes - a knee-length skirt and a pale blue blouse. Her long, dark hair is loose and wavy, falling down over her shoulders and her back, and she's wearing those cute dark-rimmed glasses she always wears to work.

She's like the epitome of the sexy librarian stereotype, and my dick instantly hardens at the sight of her.

I climb out of the car, buttoning up the front of my suit jacket and hoping that will hide the evident bulge from view at least a little bit.

"Hey," I call out to her from my driveway. "Is everything okay?"

"Yeah," she says, her cheeks turning a soft shade of pink. "I guess Mom must have had to go to the store or something and I forgot my front door key this morning. I'm just waiting for her to get home."

I sigh inwardly. I can't just leave the poor girl there when it's cold, and she's not dressed properly for the weather.

"Do you want to come and wait inside?" I offer. "You look like you're freezing."

She blushes even more and shrugs her shoulders. "I'll be fine. I don't want to be a bother."

Ellie drops her gaze to the floor, and I wonder if she's resisting because of what I said last night about it only being a one-time thing. I'm sure she would have come inside before that happened, when we were on casual speaking terms.

But I'm not going to let her stay outside in the cold. Who knows when her mom will be home. From what I've witnessed, she's unpredictable... at best. If she's gone to a bar, she might not be home until the early hours of the morning.

"Get inside," I say, resorting to that steely tone of voice she'd responded to so well last night.

As I expect, her head snaps up, and her eyes are wide when they meet mine.

"O... okay," she stutters as she rises up from the wooden stair she'd been sitting on.

It takes every bit of willpower I possess not to call her a good girl. I'm just helping her out. Like I would do with any of my neighbors. This has got nothing to do with last night.

I walk over to the front door and unlock it, holding it open for Ellie. She walks past me, her eyes darting anywhere but my face, and the sweet smell of her perfume hits me.

Damn. How the hell am I going to make it through this without doing something stupid?

I follow her inside and close the door behind us, the click of the latch loud in the awkward silence that's descended between us.

"Can I get you a drink or anything?" I ask, clearing my throat and trying to sound nonchalant.

"I'm okay, thanks," she replies, her voice soft and breathy.

She begins rubbing her hands together, blowing between them in an effort to warm them up. Without thinking, I reach out and take her hands between mine, wincing as I feel how icy-cold her fingers are.

"Damn, how long were you waiting out there?" I ask. "You're freezing."

"I don't know," she answers in a small voice. "Probably about an hour, I guess."

"Jesus, no wonder you're shivering."

Acting on instinct alone, I release her hands and unbutton my suit jacket, before pulling her towards me into a hug. She snuggles against me, wrapping her arms around my waist under my jacket, and I pull it around her as I hold her tight. Her little body is shivering against mine.

I shouldn't be doing this.

But fuck, she feels so damn good pressed against me like this.

And now my dick is hard as steel.

"Thank you, Sir," she whispers.

I clamp my lips together tightly to hold back a groan, and she stiffens in my arms, pulling back just enough that she can look up into my eyes. Her face is a deep shade of red now.

"Oh my god, I'm so sorry, Alex. That just slipped out. I won't do it again."

"You better hadn't," I say, surprised at how gruff my voice has become. "Otherwise I might have to punish you, if you do."

I'm playing with fucking fire, and I know it. But when we're alone together in my house, her body pressed up against me, I'm not sure there is enough willpower in the world to keep me away from her.

My words force a small whimper from her lips until she clamps that lower pillow of flesh between her teeth and begins nibbling on it. Her eyes slip off to the side, and it looks like she's deep in thought.

Damn it. Just when I think she can't surprise me any more, I start to suspect she has some bratty tendencies hidden away inside her.

My whole body is tense, waiting to see how she responds to the threat of a punishment. I know that if she does anything to suggest she wants to be laid across my knees for a spanking, there's no damn way I'll be able to hold back.

Not after the way I'd jerked off three times last night just thinking about the way she'd looked while I'd had her bound and helpless as I'd made her come with my fingers.

She opens her mouth, her eyes darting up to meet mine again, and the heat I see burning in her eyes is unmistakable.

"I'm sorry," she says, the tiniest hint of a smile tugging at the corners of her lips. "I'll try to be a good girl in the future... Sir."

And with that, all rational thoughts in my brain flee.

I let out a growl and crush my mouth to hers, unable to hold back any longer. My tongue demands entry, and Ellie parts her lips, letting me kiss her hard. Our tongues collide and duel with each other as she clings to me desperately, and I'm pretty sure I can feel her shaking with need.

When I pull back, she's breathless, and her pretty blue eyes are glazed over with lust.

"Now it's time for your punishment," I say, taking her hand in mine and pulling her over towards the couch.

She trips over her feet a little, but I don't slow down. I'm too eager to turn that sexy little ass of hers a bright shade of red.

We get to the sofa and I bend her over the back of it. Ellie's so damn short that she ends up on tiptoes, and I can't help but grin. She's too fucking adorable.

With rough movements, I pull her skirt up around her waist and tug her panties down to the floor, baring her ass and her pretty little cunt to me.

I take a moment to admire her glistening folds, enjoying the obvious evidence of her arousal.

"Do you know what you are being punished for, pet?" I ask, running my hand gently over her ass cheek.

"Because I called you Sir," she whimpers. "And that was just supposed to be for last night."

When I hear those words, I wince inwardly at the reminder that I'm crossing a line with her by doing this today. I'm all too aware that I could have just told her not to call me that and then dropped it. It's my fault that things have escalated once again.

But I can't help myself. There's just something about her that draws me in and refuses to let go.

"That's right," I say, using the firm tone I know she likes. "And then when I warned you it would result in a punishment if you did it again, you went ahead and called me that, anyway. So now, I'm going to turn your ass a very pretty shade of red."

She moans softly, and my cock twitches. It's already uncomfortably hard and straining painfully against my pants, and the little noises Ellie makes aren't helping matters.

"Yes, Sir," she says, helpfully pushing herself up higher on tiptoes and arching her spine to push her ass further in the air for me, putting those luscious curves on display.

Goddamn, she's practically begging for a spanking. It would be cruel to refuse her.

I lift my hand up, bringing it down in a hard slap against her pale skin. Ellie squeals, and I watch, mesmerized, as the creamy flesh turns a soft shade of pink.

"Fuck, Ellie," I mutter. "I'm going to enjoy marking up this pretty little ass."

Before she has a chance to respond, I land another stinging slap on the other cheek, and a delicious little moan falls from her lips.

"Thank you, Sir."

Jesus. The way she says those three little words has me desperate to bury my cock deep inside her. But not yet. Not until I've finished marking her skin with my handprints, so that every time she sits down for the next week, she'll know exactly who owns her ass.

Fuck, where the hell did that thought come from?

I shake my head, trying to push that particular little fantasy aside and focus on the task at hand. I've already lost control. Now, it's time to rein it back in.

So I ignore the desperate pleas of my throbbing cock and continue to spank her. I alternate between cheeks, turning them a nice, even shade of pink, and Ellie is making the most amazing noises. Every time she calls me Sir, my dick throbs and it gets harder and harder to control my desire.

Judging by the way her pussy lips are now drooling with her excitement, I can tell she's enjoying the pain. Enjoying being marked. And it makes me so damn hot.

Unable to resist any longer, I reach between her legs, sliding my fingers over her dripping folds, making Ellie whimper and squirm.

"God, you're soaked," I growl, before bringing my wet fingers to my lips and sucking on them. "And you taste fucking divine."

"Oh, please, Sir," she moans. "Please..."

I can't tell whether she's begging for more of the spanking, or begging for my fingers, so I decide to give her a little of both.

My hand smacks down against her ass once again, and Ellie lets out a cry, pushing her hips back and offering her ass to me like a greedy little brat.

She's clearly desperate for more, and I'm more than happy to give it to her. I smack her again, and again, and her cries fill the room, echoing off the walls.

I can feel the tension building inside me, and it's not just the kind that comes with the need for a release. No. There's something deeper, a tension in my chest that I've never felt before.

"Fuck," I mutter. "Your ass looks so fucking beautiful like this, pet."

Ellie moans softly, and I run my hand over her stinging flesh. The skin is warm under my touch, and I can't help but admire the way it's glowing from my attention.

But I want more.

I need to be buried deep inside her.

I move closer, my fingers brushing lightly against her folds, teasing her a little. Ellie shudders, a soft whimper escaping her lips.

"Sir, please..."

Her breathless plea sends a shiver through me, and I can't stop myself from sliding two fingers into her, filling her up.

She lets out a gasp, and her muscles clamp down around my digits, drawing me deeper inside her.

"You like that, pet?" I growl.

"Yes, Sir," she moans.

I pump my fingers in and out of her, curling them a little and brushing against that sweet spot inside her that makes her gasp.

"It feels so good, Sir. Please don't stop. Please."

Her words come out in a rush, and I can tell that she's getting close. I add a third finger, stretching her a little, and the noise that escapes her lips is almost enough to make me feral.

"Come for me, pet," I say, pumping my fingers harder and faster, making her shudder and moan.

"I... I'm so close, Sir," she says, her voice coming out breathy.

"Good girl. Don't hold back. Give me what I need. Come for me now."

I curl my fingers, hitting that perfect spot inside her, and Ellie cries out, her body going taut as her muscles clench around my fingers.

"Sir!" she screams, her whole body trembling.

I don't let up, my fingers moving faster and harder, fucking her through her orgasm. She's so wet, her juices are running down my wrist and soaking into my sleeve, and the sounds she's making are driving me insane.

"Good girl," I say, my voice low and gravelly. "Such a good girl."

When she finally comes down from her high, her legs give out and she collapses against the back of the couch. Her whole body is trembling, and I can't resist pulling her into my arms, holding her tightly against my chest.

"I think you enjoyed your spanking, didn't you, pet?" I murmur, my lips brushing against her ear.

"Yes, Sir," she sighs, her voice barely audible. "It was amazing."

"Good." I drop a kiss to the top of her head. "I'm glad."

There's a long moment of silence, and I'm content to just hold her, feeling her body pressed against mine. It's a strange sensation. It's not something I'm used to.

But the moment is ruined by the sound of a car outside, and as we both turn to look out the front window, we see her mom's car pulling into their driveway.

"Damn it," she says, pulling away from me and smoothing down her skirt. "I'm so sorry, Alex, but I should go. Mom will be mad if I stay here too long."

I frown, wondering how the hell Ellie's mom has still got such a hold over her when she's an adult. But before I can figure out the best way to ask her about it, she's gone.

With a sigh, I glance down and realize her panties are still on the floor behind the couch, and I bend to pick them up. At least I'll have a little reminder of Ellie later when I'm trying to relieve this pent up frustration I'm feeling.

Chapter Five

Ellie:

"And where were you?" Mom asks the second I rush through the front door, only a couple of minutes after she'd arrived home.

She turns to look at me, and I don't even have to get close to her to smell the alcohol on her breath. It's pungent and overwhelming, and it makes my stomach churn.

For a moment, all I can do is hate the man who turned her into this shell of a woman. But honestly, I hate her a little too for allowing it to happen. This has been my fucking life ever since I was fifteen, and I'm sick of it. I want to get out, but with the house prices being so high, I can't afford anything by myself. Although I have been saving every spare cent for the last few months, so hopefully I won't have to put up with this too much longer.

"I was just next door," I say, trying to keep my voice casual. "I forgot my front door key this morning so I couldn't get in. Alex let me wait inside because it was so cold out there."

At the mere mention of his name, I feel my face start to heat up.

I'm still reeling from what we'd done. And not just the fact that he'd spanked me, but also the fact that we'd both enjoyed it so much. I can still feel the sting on my ass, and it sends a wave of excitement through me.

Mom takes a step closer, looking me in the eye. "Be careful, Ellie," she says. "I'm sure he'd fuck you in a heartbeat if he could. And I've already told you, men are trouble. They'll break your heart, then leave you all alone."

"I know, Mom," I say with a sigh. "You tell me that every day. But, you know, not all men are like…"

"Don't you dare say his name in my house," she shouts, interrupting me before I can finish and smacking her hand down hard enough on the kitchen table that the loud noise makes me flinch. "Why are you even defending him, Ellie?"

"I'm not," I say, feeling the frustration rising within me. "I don't care about him. But I'd also just like to be able to live my life for once without you telling me what to do. I'm an adult, for god's sake, and I don't see why I should have to pay for things that were done to you in the past by other people."

With each word, my voice rises until I'm shouting right back at her. My heart is hammering inside my chest, and I can feel myself trembling. I don't think she'd ever hurt me - she never has in the past - but I'm tired of living like this, scared of her all the time.

Mom looks at me, her eyes narrowing, and I have a feeling I might be about to regret what I did.

"Is something going on between you and the guy next door? Is that why you're acting like this all of a sudden?"

"No, Mom," I say with a sigh.

And it's not exactly a lie. Alex made it clear last night that he's not interested in a relationship with me. Or with anyone.

"If I find out you're fucking him, Ellie, you'll be out of this house in a heartbeat. I know you don't understand this, but I'm just doing this to protect you. I love you so much, baby, and I never want you to have to experience what I went through."

She's sniffling now, her eyes glistening with tears, and I know I should feel something other than disgust when she steps closer and strokes my cheek with an unsteady hand. But this is her usual pattern. Getting mad at me for doing nothing, then turning on the waterworks to try and make me feel bad.

It took me way too long to realize this is her way of manipulating me into doing exactly what she wants. But I'm not playing this game anymore.

I take a step back, removing myself from her reach, and her expression darkens.

"I'm not fucking him, Mom. I can promise you that. But I'm going to my room. I don't want to have this conversation again."

"So little fucking respect for me," I hear her mutter as she goes to the shopping bags she'd left on the floor when she got home. Unsurprisingly, she pulls out a bottle of beer, pops the cap off, and takes a long drink.

"After everything I've done for her and she still can't give me the slightest bit of damn respect. The ungrateful little bitch."

Even though she is mumbling the words to herself, they still hurt, and I turn and head to my bedroom before she can see the tears in my eyes.

I'm so done with this.

But at the same time, I'm trapped here.

Until I have enough money to move out, anyway, and who knows how long that's going to take. I'm reliant on Mom's money for survival, and she knows it.

My dad had passed away when I was only five, and I don't remember him too well. But apparently he had been very successful, running the financial investment business he'd set up with his brother. He'd left Mom a lot of money when he'd died, and with the help of my uncle investing it wisely, it means Mom will never have to work again. Hell, she can't even drink enough to get through the interest she earns on the money.

But, of course, she won't let me see a damn cent of it. She wants me to stay here with her. She wants me to be completely dependent on her, because then she can control me. It's all she ever does - using her money and her temper tantrums and her emotional manipulation to keep me under her thumb.

A tear falls down onto my cheek as I think about how trapped I am here. But not for much longer. I'm doing what I can to get out. I just have to be patient while I save my money.

And in the meantime, at least I have my fantasies about Alex. That's the only thing that has been keeping me feeling sane ever since he first moved in next door.

I purposely turn my thoughts to how it had felt tonight as he'd spanked my ass, and how good it had felt as he'd fingered me to an intense orgasm.

These are the kinds of thoughts that bring a sense of peace, even as they create a heat between my thighs for even more of his touch.

Alex is the one person in my life who has ever made me feel good. And as much as I know he doesn't want anything serious, I still can't help wanting him.

Even though I know that can never happen. Between his reluctance to be in a relationship, and my mom's crazy attempts to make sure I never date anyone, it feels impossible.

But if the only way I can have him is through fantasy, then so be it.

I close my eyes, picturing his strong, muscular body. I haven't even seen him naked, but I already know that he's perfection. Those broad shoulders, those bulging biceps, and those hands that feel so big and powerful. The way he'd picked me up so easily last night at the club just goes to show how strong he is.

God, I'm already getting wet again.

I run my own hands over my breasts, imagining it's Alex touching me.

My nipples are already hard, and as I pinch them through my clothes, I picture him above me.

I imagine it's his fingers sliding over my stomach, his palms gliding over my hips.

My heart is racing, and my pussy is throbbing, and the need for release is overwhelming.

My hand slides under my skirt, and I let out a soft gasp as I realize my panties are gone. I must have left them at Alex's place when I rushed out. Oh god, it's going to be so embarrassing if he finds them. But at the same time, there's a part of me that loves the idea of him holding onto something of mine.

Maybe even using them to pleasure himself.

That thought makes me even hotter, and as I slip a finger into my dripping wet pussy, I can't help but wish it was Alex's fingers instead.

"Fuck," I whisper, pushing a second finger inside myself.

I can't even think about him without being consumed by this aching need for him.

And I know it's wrong. He doesn't want me like that. And he doesn't want a relationship.

But, god, I want him so much.

My fingers slide in and out, and I can feel myself getting closer to the edge.

"Oh, Alex," I moan, and the words slips from my lips before I can stop them.

But it feels so good. It feels right.

And as I imagine him touching me, whispering to me, calling me his good girl, I fall apart.

"Oh, god," I whimper, as my pussy clenches around my fingers.

My orgasm crashes over me, and as the pleasure consumes my body, I can't help thinking how amazing it would feel to have Alex's cock buried inside me as I come.

I want him. I want him so fucking badly.

And as the orgasm fades away, leaving me gasping and shaking, I realize there's no point trying to deny it.

I have fallen hard for Alex, and no matter how hard I try, I can't get him out of my head.

He's the one man who makes me feel alive. He's the one man who makes me feel loved.

And the one man who can never be mine.

But how am I supposed to stop craving him as much as I do? It's impossible.

Chapter Six

Alex:

I take a sip of my coffee as I peek out the front window again. After the way Ellie ran out on me last night, I'm still curious about what the hell is going on between her and her mom. Sure, I've heard some shouting coming from their house at times, always from the mother, but the panic on Ellie's face when she'd seen her mom pull up outside their house was unmistakable.

Worry churns in the pit of my stomach, making me feel nauseous.

I'm determined to get to the bottom of whatever is going on, just to make sure she is safe. If she isn't, well, then I will have to do something to fix it.

It hits me like a punch to the gut that I've fallen for her already. The worry I feel for her is so much more than just neighborly concern. I barely slept last night as I tossed and turned in bed, the memory of Ellie's panicked expression etched in my memory.

I need to leave for work soon, but I'm hoping to see Ellie before I do, just to make sure she's okay.

A movement from outside catches my eye, and as I look up, I see Ellie walking towards her car. I quickly put my mug down on the nearby table and rush out the front door to catch up with her.

"Hey, Ellie," I call out as I jog towards her.

Her posture stiffens, and she turns around slowly to look at me. "Hi," she says, her lips curling up into a forced smile.

I run my gaze over her from top to bottom, and this time, it's not because I'm checking her out. I need to make sure she's unharmed.

She's wearing a dark gray pencil skirt and a pastel pink blouse. Her long, dark brown hair is pulled back in a loose ponytail, and she's wearing the cute glasses she always wears to work. She's beautiful, as always. And there aren't any obvious signs that she's been hurt.

But her eyes keep darting towards her house, and her posture is rigid.

"Are you okay?" I ask, stepping closer.

"Umm, yeah, of course," she says, nodding her head as if that little movement will convince me that she's telling the truth. "But I'm running late for work, so I can't stop and chat. Have a good day, Alex."

"You too," I say, as I watch her back up towards her car and get inside.

I want to stop her, and demand to know what's going on, so that I can help her if she is in trouble. But I know this isn't the right time or place. Ellie was obviously worried about her mom seeing us talking, and if I force her to stay with me any longer, I might end up making her situation at home worse, rather than better.

So I take a step back and turn, walking towards my house as I quickly formulate a plan in my mind.

If it's not safe to talk to her here, I'll go see her at work instead. At least she won't have to worry about us being seen together there, and she might be able to talk to me a little more freely. I already know she works in a library, and while she's never told me which one specifically, there are only two libraries locally, so it shouldn't take long to find her.

As I close my front door behind me, I pull my phone out of my jacket pocket and begin typing an email to my secretary, telling her that I won't be in to work today and that I need her to reschedule my meetings.

There's no way I'd be able to concentrate at work until I'm certain Ellie is safe, anyway. I need to take care of my girl.

That's more important than anything else right now.

*****

An hour later, I park my car outside the second library in the area and head inside. The first one I went to was a dead end, so this has to be the one she works at.

The smell of books is the first thing that hits me as I walk through the large double doors.

The walls are lined with floor-to-ceiling shelves, and each shelf is full to the brim with books.

At the far end of the room is a large children's section, and there are a few small kids running around, grabbing books off the shelves and taking them over to the large beanbags that are spread throughout the area.

A little further towards the left is a small section full of computers, and the middle of the room is taken up by a handful of long tables and chairs. There are people sitting around the tables, either working on laptops or reading books, and as I glance around the rest of the room, I notice several others sitting in comfortable armchairs scattered around the place.

I smile to myself. I can imagine Ellie being happy working in a place like this. It's a nice, relaxing atmosphere.

As I walk further into the building, I catch sight of Ellie standing behind a counter, talking to a couple of older women. Her eyes are bright, and her cheeks are flushed, and when she laughs at something one of the women says, it makes me smile. She looks so happy. So relaxed.

She must sense me watching her, because a moment later, she turns her head and our eyes meet. Her jaw drops open, and her eyes widen, but then her cheeks flush a darker shade of red, and a hint of a smile appears on her lips.

Fuck, when she looks at me like that, it's all I can do to not cross the room and kiss her until she's breathless.

She excuses herself and walks over to me.

"What are you doing here, Alex?" she asks, and her tone is full of surprise.

"I just wanted to check on you," I say, glancing around. "I was worried about you after the way you left in such a hurry last night. And this morning."

Her face brightens, and she tilts her head before she begins walking behind one of the large bookshelves. I follow her.

"I'm really sorry about that," she says, her gaze lowering to the floor. "It's just that my mom... well, how do I explain this? She has issues with men. And whenever she thinks a guy might be interested in me, she tends to go a little crazy about it."

Ellie looks up at me again, a small, embarrassed smile on her lips.

"Sometimes, I'd much prefer to avoid the drama with her, you know? So I'm trying not to make it look like there is more to our friendship than there really is."

I nod and take a quick look around to make sure we're out of sight before backing Ellie up into one of the corners. A small gasp escapes her, and I reach out to grip onto a metal shelf either side of her head. If I don't hold on to something, I'm not sure I'm going to be able to resist touching her. And I should behave myself when I'm visiting her at work.

"Okay, I can understand that completely. But what do you mean when you say it makes your mom go a little crazy? Does she...?"

I let my words trail off, not sure if I can bring myself to say them.

Her eyes widen and she shakes her head. "She's never hurt me, if that's what you're asking. She just shouts a lot, that's all."

Ellie reaches out and puts a hand on my chest, and her touch sends a bolt of heat through me.

"Honestly, she's just a little dramatic. Please don't worry about me. I'm fine."

Her eyes slip away from mine, and for a moment, I wonder if she's still hiding something. But then she's looking at me again, and there is so much heat in her gaze that it suddenly becomes difficult to think about anything other than leaning down to capture her lips in a kiss.

The corners of her mouth curve up into a sexy little smile, and she tilts her head up towards me, as if she wants me to kiss her.

She licks her lips, and I groan, unable to hold back any longer.

I lower my lips to hers, and as soon as they touch, I'm lost.

Her taste, her smell, her soft whimpers. It's all intoxicating, and the way her tongue feels sliding against mine drives me wild.

Unable to resist, I press my body against hers, pushing her back against the shelves behind her. I can't seem to get enough.

Ellie moans softly, and she grips the lapels of my jacket, pulling me even closer.

It takes every ounce of self-control I have not to strip her naked and take her right here, up against the bookshelves.

Fuck, why did I have to think about her naked? Now I can't get the image out of my head, and it makes my cock harden painfully in my pants.

This woman is driving me insane, and all I want to do is claim her as mine.

I thought I could keep my distance from her. Thought I could just toy with my innocent younger neighbor for one night and then walk away. But it's impossible.

When I'm not with her, she's all I can think about. And when I'd thought there was something wrong, I'd found it impossible to eat or sleep. Hell, I even took a day off work for her today, and I can't remember the last time I called out of work.

Ellie is unlike anyone I've ever met before. She's sweet and sexy and so fucking innocent. She's a temptation that I can't resist.

"Alex," she whispers against my lips. "We can't do this here. If my boss sees me, I might get fired."

Her words bring me back to my senses, and I back up a step or two. Ellie's breathing hard, and her lips are red and swollen from my kisses.

God, she looks so beautiful.

"You're right, I'm sorry. That's the last thing I want to happen."

Ellie bites her lip, and her cheeks turn a darker shade of red. "I have a lunch break at 12," she says. "Maybe we could meet up somewhere then?"

She looks up at me from under her eyelashes, and the way her shy smile makes her dimples appear is adorable.

Fuck, how did I manage to resist her for so long?

"Come to Club Surrender at twelve," I tell her. Maybe I should take her out for something to eat, but right now, I only have an appetite for one thing. And it's not food. "It's closed until tonight, so we'll have the place to ourselves."

I lean in, pressing my lips to hers one more time before backing away and heading for the exit.

"Oh, and Ellie," I add, stopping to glance back at her.

She's still leaning against the bookshelves, her hand pressed against her lips, and a dreamy look on her face.

"Don't wear any panties," I say, and then leave before she can respond.

My cock is already rock hard, and if I don't leave now, I'm going to have to do something about it.

Like bend her over one of the library tables and fuck her right here and now.

I'm not sure how much longer I can hold out. I want her so fucking badly. And the more time I spend with her, the harder it is to resist.

I need some time alone with her so we can discuss what we both want and need from this. Especially with the added complications her mom brings.

And maybe, if I'm lucky, by the end of the day, I will be able to find out if this is as intense for her as it is for me.

Chapter Seven

Ellie:

I stand outside Surrender, wondering if I should knock. Would Alex even hear me if I did? The club is huge and he might not be close enough to the door to hear me.

A strange mix of nerves and excitement swirl around in the pit of my stomach, making me feel slightly nauseous, but in a good way, if that's even possible. Why would Alex bring me to his BDSM club when it's closed if he didn't want something to happen between us today? And why would he tell me not to wear panties? My entire body is aching for his touch, and I'm hopeful I might get it today.

Just as I lift my hand to try knocking, the door swings open and Alex is standing in the doorway, a crooked grin on his lips.

"I've been watching you on the camera for the last five minutes, wondering if you're going to come in," he says, a teasing tone lacing his words.

My face grows hot and I giggle nervously. "Sorry, I wasn't sure if I should knock or just come in," I explain.

He opens the door wider and steps back, giving me space to enter. "Oh, you should definitely come in," he says, and when my eyes meet his, there's a hunger in his gaze that sends a shiver of desire straight through me.

As I step into the club, he closes the door behind me and leans in close. His scent surrounds me, making my head spin, and when his fingers graze my arm, my skin tingles where he touches.

"I hope you did as you were told and came here without panties," he whispers, his voice low and husky.

My nipples harden under my thin blouse, and my body trembles. I nod my head slowly, so overwhelmed with my need for him that I can't find any words.

"Show me," he says, the tone of his voice making it clear he expects to be obeyed immediately.

With trembling fingers, I tug my tight pencil skirt up around my waist and he moves back a step, his eyes lingering on the smooth skin between my thighs.

His hand reaches out, and his fingers brush along my pussy, making my breath hitch.

"Good girl," he growls. "I'm looking forward to seeing how many times I can make you come during your lunch break. But first, we need to have a little talk. Come with me, pet, and don't bother pulling your skirt down. There's nobody here but us, and I like seeing you with your pretty pussy on display for me."

He gently takes my hand, and we begin walking through to the main room of the club.

"Umm, about that," I begin, and I'm surprised to hear how shaky and breathless I already sound. "I told my boss that I had a bad headache and that I wouldn't be back at work this afternoon."

Alex stops in his tracks, looking down at me with a wicked grin tugging at the corners of his lips.

"You mean to say I have several hours to make you come repeatedly for me, Ellie?"

"Yes, Sir," I whimper.

The way he looks at me, like he wants to devour me, is intoxicating, and all I want is to give him whatever he desires.

Alex groans and cups the side of my face in his hand. He lowers his lips to mine, kissing me with an intensity that leaves me breathless.

When he finally breaks away, his eyes are dark and full of lust, and my heart pounds against my ribs.

"Fuck, you're gorgeous, Ellie. I can't wait to taste that sweet little pussy of yours. Come with me, pet."

I follow him over to one of the leather sofas that line the walls of the club and he sits down, tugging me into his lap. With a gasp, I try to bounce straight back up again, but Alex stops me with one strong arm around my waist.

"What's the matter, Ellie? You don't want to sit in my lap?"

My face burns, and I struggle to meet his gaze. "It's not that, Alex. But your suit must cost more than I make in a year, and I don't want to make a mess of it."

Alex chuckles, but doesn't release his hold on me. "If you're wet enough to make a mess of my pants just from sitting in my lap, then that will be worth every fucking cent of the dry cleaning bill."

I whimper and nod, relaxing a little. It's only then that I realize how hard he is. His erection presses against my ass cheeks, and when I wriggle a little in his lap, he groans.

"Before I start getting too distracted," he says, gathering my hair in his fist and tilting my head so I'm forced to look up into his eyes, "I have to confess something, pet. I made a bit of a mistake with you on our first night together."

"Oh," I say, trying to swallow past the sudden lump in my throat.

I don't like the sound of where this conversation is going.

"Yes," he continues, his eyes searching mine. "I told you that I only wanted one night. And I told myself that would be enough to satisfy my curiosity about you. But apparently that was a mistake."

"Oh," I gasp.

He slides his free hand up my side to gently cup my breast, then brushes his thumb casually back and forth across my nipple, making the little bud pebble under his touch.

"I suspect you feel the same way, pet. But I'm concerned about your mom. I don't want to do anything that might put you in harm's way with her."

"No, Alex," I murmur, struggling to concentrate with his hands all over me. "You won't. She doesn't need to know. I'm twenty-three, Alex, and I'm sick and tired of letting her run my life because she's worried I'll get hurt like she was."

One corner of his lip curls upwards into an amused little smile. "I'd get to be your dirty little secret? That could be fun."

I squirm some more in his lap, feeling his cock harden even more as I do, and he lets out a low growl.

"Seeing as we have more time than I thought, tell me a bit more about your mom and why she acts the way she does."

I let out a soft sigh and shrug.

"There was this guy," I say. "Mom met him when I was about twelve, and she was smitten with him straight away. I can remember she kept telling me about how perfect he was, and how she never thought she'd find anyone else after my dad died. She was happier than I'd ever seen her before, and I knew she had plans to marry him, even though he hadn't asked her yet."

I pause and take a breath, but Alex remains silent, his eyes locked on my face as if he's hanging on every word. Such direct attention causes a little flutter of excitement between my thighs, and I continue, hoping to get this part over with quickly so we can get to the part where he promised to make me come repeatedly.

"They dated for three years, and he still hadn't proposed to Mom. He'd come round to see her or take her out maybe two or three evenings a week, but he'd never stay the night. So she started getting suspicious and doing some digging around."

Alex's lips narrow, and I have a feeling he knows where this story is going.

"It turned out he was already married and had a whole other family he'd never told her about. He had kids and everything. Mom ended it, but it broke something inside her. And ever since, she's always done her best to drill it into me that I should avoid men because they are all assholes."

He nods and reaches up to cup my face in both his hands. "That guy did a shitty thing to her. And my father cheated on my mother repeatedly when I was younger, until she found out and threw him out, so I know how much cheating can ruin a family."

"I'm sorry," I whisper, feeling a dull ache in my chest that his father had done that to him and his mom.

He shakes his head and continues. "But I'm not anything like your mom's ex. And I would never do anything to hurt you."

His words make me melt inside, and I start squirming in his lap again.

"You won't?" I ask, unable to stop the playful grin that teases the corners of my lips. "Because the spanking you gave me last night hurt, but I was hoping you might do it again one day, Sir."

A low growl rumbles through him, and he slides one hand down my body to cup one of my ass cheeks in his hand. "Don't worry, pet. I can see many spankings in your future. And I'll make sure you enjoy every single damn one of them. But, I promise you, I will never hurt you in a way you don't enjoy."

"I believe you, Alex," I whisper. "But you have to know something else."

"Oh?"

I lick my lips and lean in closer. "I've never been with a man before," I say, the words coming out as a whisper. "I've never let anyone else touch me or kiss me. Until you, Alex. You're the first."

"Fuck," he hisses, and his arms wrap tightly around me, pulling me against his chest. "I had a feeling that would be the case, considering how your mom feels about you dating, but hearing it confirmed..."

He trails off, his voice choked with emotion, and his mouth crashes down on mine. His tongue sweeps across the seam of my lips and I part them for him, moaning softly when our tongues dance together.

I press my body tighter against his, desperate to feel every inch of him. His arms are firm and strong around me, holding me securely.

And suddenly, I feel safe and protected in a way that I've never felt before.

I lose myself in the kiss, letting it consume me. When his lips leave mine and move lower, trailing a hot line of kisses along my neck, I moan.

"Please, Sir," I whimper. "I need more."

"Don't worry, pet," he growls. "You'll get everything you need."

He rises up from the couch, holding me in his arms. "But we should go somewhere more private, in case one of my friends comes in before opening time. I want you all to myself, pet."

I whimper and nod, nuzzling my face against the side of his neck as he carries me through the club and into the quiet back area, where he took me on my first night at the club.

This is it.

Alex is going to take my virginity. And my entire body is buzzing with excitement and anticipation.

I've fantasized about this moment for so long, and it's finally going to become a reality.

Chapter Eight

Ellie:

As soon as Alex shuts the door to the private room, his lips are claiming mine in a hungry kiss. I'm still in his arms, and I wrap my arms and legs around the solid bulk of his muscular body, clinging to him desperately.

"God, Ellie," he murmurs against my lips. "I can't keep my hands off you."

"Then don't," I breathe. "Please, Alex, I need you to touch me."

His low groan echoes through the quiet room, and he pulls me tighter against him, deepening the kiss while he backs me up against the nearest wall.

As his tongue delves deeper into my mouth, his hands slide up the backs of my thighs, stopping just shy of my ass. My tight skirt is still hitched up above my waist, and with his command to meet him without panties, my ass and pussy are fully exposed.

I whimper and squirm, grinding myself against his erection, which is rock hard and pressing against me.

"Fuck, pet," he growls, breaking away from the kiss and burying his face against the side of my neck.

"I've thought about this moment ever since that first night you came to the club," he admits. "You've been driving me wild, and I don't think I can resist you much longer."

His confession makes my heart flutter in my chest, happiness surging through me as I find out he needs me just as badly as I need him.

I don't care what my mom thinks about me dating him. I love him. And I don't want to live without him. If anything, this is just making me even more determined to get out of her house as quickly as possible.

"I don't want you to resist, Sir," I tell him, gasping and grinding harder against his cock. "I need you so badly. Please."

He groans and grips my ass cheeks tightly, his fingers biting into my flesh, and the slight pain is intoxicating.

"You're so damn sweet and eager, pet," he growls. "I need to taste your pretty little pussy."

I let out a squeal as he spins us both around, and then he sets me down on my feet.

"Strip," he commands, then he takes a step back, his gaze roaming up and down my body as if he's trying to devour me with nothing but his eyes.

The hunger in his expression makes my entire body tingle, and I reach up to unbutton my blouse, revealing the lacy white bra beneath.

He sucks in a sharp breath, his eyes drinking in the sight of me as I shrug the blouse off and drop it to the floor. Then I slowly lower the zipper on my skirt, tugging it down and letting it fall to the floor as well.

"God, you're stunning, pet," Alex says. "You're the most beautiful woman I've ever seen."

My cheeks flush, and a rush of excitement swells between my thighs.

"Thank you, Sir," I whisper.

When he nods his head, gesturing for me to continue, I reach back and unfasten my bra, letting the straps slide down my arms before tossing the scrap of lace aside.

My nipples are already stiff and aching, and they pebble even more when Alex groans.

"Take your hair down, pet," he orders, his voice deep and husky. "I want to see it cascading around your shoulders."

With trembling fingers, I reach up and pull out the hair tie that had been keeping the long strands captured in a pony tail.

As my hair falls down, brushing against my shoulders, Alex closes the distance between us and gathers a handful of the dark locks, winding them around his fist.

He pulls my head back, making me gasp, and lowers his lips to mine. His tongue plunges into my mouth, and the kiss is demanding, almost punishing, and it makes me wetter and needier for him than ever before.

His free hand cups one of my breasts, his thumb brushing across my nipple, and then he pinches the tender bud lightly, sending sparks of pleasure rushing through me.

I moan into his mouth and arch my back, thrusting my chest forward, silently begging for more.

"Please, Sir," I manage to mumble, though the words are muffled by his lips.

Alex growls and pulls back. "Do you want my mouth on your pretty little nipples, pet?"

"Yes," I whimper. "Yes, please, Alex."

He chuckles and releases my hair. "Such good manners, Ellie. You're such a good girl."

With his eyes locked on mine, he leans down and licks one of my nipples, and a shudder runs through me. Then he wraps his lips around it and sucks it into his mouth, flicking his tongue back and forth over the little nub, and I moan, tangling my fingers in his hair and holding him against me.

His mouth feels amazing, and I'm desperate for more. I need to feel his hands on every part of me, his mouth on every inch of my body.

Alex wraps his arms around me and lifts me up, keeping his mouth on my breast as he carries me over to the bed. He lays me down gently and stands up straight, his gaze raking up and down my body.

"I can't get enough of you," he growls. "I'm so fucking hungry for you, pet."

He kneels at the edge of the bed and tugs me towards him, draping my legs over his shoulders. The position leaves me completely open and exposed to him, and a surge of heat rushes to my core.

"Fuck," Alex growls. "Your sweet little cunt is so pink and pretty. And so wet."

Before I can respond, his head dips down and his mouth covers me, his tongue delving between my slick folds.

"Oh, fuck!" I gasp, the words turning into a loud moan as he begins eating me out with a ferocity that's almost animalistic.

His tongue dances over my clit, teasing me mercilessly, and when he slides two fingers deep inside me, I cry out, writhing and bucking on the bed.

"You taste so good, Ellie," he growls, lifting his head just long enough to meet my gaze. "So fucking good."

"Please," I beg. "Please, Sir. I'm so close. Make me come. Please!"

He grins at me with lips coated in my wetness, then ducks his head back down and flicks his tongue over my clit again.

"Come for me, pet," he growls.

I cry out and arch my back, the tension inside me snapping. Pleasure ripples through me in wave after wave, and my pussy clenches and spasms around his fingers as he keeps licking and sucking on my sensitive little nub.

My vision goes dark, and for a moment, I feel like I'm floating. My entire body is trembling and tingling, and my mind is blissfully empty.

When the pleasure finally begins to subside, Alex pulls back, his lips and chin glistening with my juices.

"Fuck, pet," he groans, licking his lips. "You have the sweetest pussy I've ever tasted."

"Oh, Sir," I whisper, my voice shaky and my breathing uneven. "That was... wow."

"That was just the beginning, pet," he tells me, his voice thick with lust. "I'm not even close to being finished with you yet."

Alex begins pumping his fingers slowly in and out of me, and I let out a moan.

"This is my pretty little pussy now, Ellie. It belongs to me. Nobody else has ever touched you here before, and nobody else ever will. But now, I think it's time for me to claim it properly."

The possessiveness in his words sends a thrill through me, and I nod eagerly, a whimper escaping my lips.

"Yes, Sir," I whisper. "It's yours. All yours."

Alex removes his fingers, and the loss of his touch is almost painful. But I know what's coming next, and my entire body quivers in anticipation.

He rises up from his position at the foot of the bed, and his hands go to his suit jacket. He slides the expensive garment off and tosses it aside, and then he begins unbuttoning his shirt.

My eyes are glued to him as his hands move down, and I suck in a sharp breath as his bare chest is revealed.

His torso is even more impressive than I'd imagined. Hard muscles ripple beneath his tanned skin, and a smattering of hair covers his pecs.

My eyes trail lower, and I watch as he undoes his pants and pushes them and his boxer briefs down his hips.

When his cock springs free, my mouth falls open, and my pussy clenches with need.

It's even bigger and thicker than I'd thought it would be, and it's rock hard; the head of his cock flushed with arousal and dripping with precum.

"Alex," I whimper, feeling a rush of anxiety and excitement at the thought of taking his cock.

"Don't worry, Ellie," he soothes, his voice soft. "I'll take care of you. I'm going to make you feel so good, pet."

I nod, trusting him. He'll make sure I'm okay.

Alex climbs onto the bed, his weight making the mattress dip, and he crawls up until his body is stretched out over mine. His lips capture mine, and I can taste myself on him, the reminder of the way he made me come flooding me with fresh desire.

His cock is nestled against my pussy, and as he kisses me, his hips roll and grind against me, rubbing his hard length through my slick folds.

The feeling of his thick shaft sliding through my wetness makes me moan, and my hips begin rocking against his.

"I'm not going to make you wait anymore, pet," he murmurs, pulling back to look at me. "Are you ready for my cock?"

"Please, yes," I gasp, nodding eagerly. "I'm ready, Sir."

Alex's gaze locks with mine, and his eyes are blazing with intensity as he reaches down and guides his cock to my entrance.

"Fuck," he growls, his eyes squeezing shut as he starts pushing his thick cock inside me. "You're so fucking tight, pet. Your sweet little pussy is strangling my cock."

He pushes deeper, stretching me open, and there's a twinge of pain, but it's quickly overtaken by the pleasure of having him inside me.

"Are you okay, Ellie?" he asks, his voice strained as he stills halfway inside me.

"Yes, Sir," I whisper.

"Good girl," he growls.

Then he thrusts forward, sheathing his entire length inside me in one swift movement.

A cry rips from my lips, and I gasp at the feeling of him buried deep inside me, stretching and filling me in a way that's so intense, it almost hurts.

"Shh, shh, you're okay," Alex murmurs, pressing his forehead against mine. "You're okay, Ellie. Just relax."

I nod, doing my best to relax and adjust to his size. The discomfort slowly fades, replaced by a feeling of fullness and pleasure; and when I begin moving my hips against him, grinding myself against his cock, Alex lets out a groan.

"That's my good girl," he breathes. "I'm going to move now, Ellie. I'm going to claim your pussy as mine. Are you ready, pet?"

"Yes, Sir," I reply, nodding eagerly. "Please, I need you."

He kisses me, his lips searing hot against mine, and then he pulls back, his eyes locking with mine.

"Tell me who you belong to, pet," he growls, his tone deep and commanding.

"You, Sir," I gasp. "I'm yours."

"Fuck," he snarls, and he pulls his hips back, slowly withdrawing from me before thrusting back inside.

The sudden movement makes me cry out, and I wrap my arms around his neck, clinging to him tightly.

"Tell me again," he orders, his voice rough and strained.

"I'm yours, Sir," I repeat, the words barely more than a breathless whisper.

Alex begins thrusting in and out of me, each stroke slow and deliberate, and I cling to him, whimpering and moaning as the pressure and pleasure build.

"You're so fucking tight, Ellie," he groans. "So wet and tight and perfect. You were made for me, pet."

I can only gasp and nod, lost in the incredible sensations of having him moving inside me.

He thrusts harder and faster, and I can tell that he's losing control, his movements becoming more urgent.

"Fuck, Ellie," he growls. "Your tight little pussy feels so good. I'm not going to last much longer. Come for me, pet. Come all over my cock."

His hand drops between our bodies, his fingers finding my clit and rubbing the swollen nub. The extra stimulation is enough to push me over the edge, and I scream out his name as my orgasm crashes over me.

"Fuck, Ellie," he growls, and with one final, powerful thrust, he buries his cock deep inside me and comes.

I can feel his cock throbbing and twitching, and his warm release floods my core.

We both shudder and shake as our orgasms wrack our bodies, and it's like nothing I've ever experienced before.

When it's finally over, Alex collapses on top of me, burying his face against the crook of my neck and shoulder.

"Fuck, Ellie," he murmurs, his voice low and husky. "That was..."

"Perfect," I finish for him, my own voice hoarse and shaky.

"Yeah," he agrees, pressing a kiss against my neck. "So fucking perfect."

I close my eyes, feeling totally spent and blissfully content.

"I love you," I whisper, then I clamp my lips tightly shut as I realize what I just said. But it's too late to take the words back now.

Oh god. How could I be so stupid and ruin such an amazing moment? If he doesn't feel the same, then he might not ever want to see me again.

Alex pulls back to meet my gaze, his eyes dark and intense as he stares down at me. My heart is hammering so hard against my rib cage that I swear he must be able to hear it.

"I love you, too," he says, his lips curving up into a wide smile.

I grin back at him, wrapping my arms and legs around him, pulling him close and clinging to him like I never want to let him go.

Because that's the last thing I ever want to do.

Chapter Nine

Alex:

I stroke Ellie's hair back from her face while I watch her sleep peacefully, her head resting on my bare chest.

Shit, despite my insistence on our first night together that I could keep this whole thing under control, I've fallen hard and fast for her. The feel of her warm little body tucked in against mine gives me a feeling of peace unlike anything else I've ever felt.

I'm forty-six, and maybe it's time to put the childhood trauma behind me. My dad was a piece of shit who treated my mother badly, but I'm not going to be like him. I'm going to do everything in my power to love and protect Ellie until the day I die.

A glance at the clock tells me it's only an hour before Ellie would usually be home from work, and I need to make sure she doesn't get home later than usual. The last thing I want is to cause trouble between her and her mom.

That is something I plan to fix, but I need time to do that. And in the meantime, I don't want to cause any extra drama for my pretty pet.

I tilt my head down and begin covering her face with gentle kisses, not stopping until she begins waking. Her eyelids flutter open and a smile spreads across her lips as her eyes land on my face.

"Hello, gorgeous," I say, running my fingers through her hair. "How are you feeling?"

"Amazing," she replies, her voice sleepy.

"Good," I tell her, smiling back at her. "But I'm afraid we need to get you home soon, pet. We don't want your mom to suspect anything."

"Oh," she says, a disappointed look flashing across her face. "But I like it here, Sir."

She snuggles closer and begins kissing and suckling at the sensitive skin on the side of my neck.

"Keep doing that," I growl, "and I'll be sending you home with an ass so red you'll be lucky if you can sit down for the next week."

My words cause her to whimper, the needy little sounds sending a rush of blood straight down to my dick.

"I'm going to miss you, Alex," she says, her plump lips forming the most adorable little pout.

"I'll miss you too, Ellie. But it's important that you get home on time. I have an idea of something that might help while we're apart, though."

"Oh?" she asks, the pout suddenly gone as she lifts her head from my chest and looks down at me. "What is it?"

I chuckle. "Let me get it for you. I'm certain you're going to enjoy it."

I untangle myself from the mess of limbs and climb out of the bed, walking over to a dresser and opening one of the drawers. It only takes me a second to find what I need, and when I turn back towards to bed, the expression on Ellie's face is one of pure lust. Her eyes have dropped down to my cock, and she's licking her lips.

Fuck, if she keeps looking at me like that, I might have to throw all caution to the wind and keep her here so I can fuck her relentlessly for hours.

I walk back to her, enjoying the way she gasps as my dick swings between my legs with each step.

"Such a greedy girl," I say as I sit down on the edge of the bed, gripping her chin so I can tilt her head up and make her look into my eyes. "You only had my cock a little while ago, but I think you need it again already, don't you, pet?"

Her cheeks redden and she nods, causing a smirk to spread across my face.

"I know, pet. And if we had the time, I would give you what you want right now. But I've got this for you instead."

I pull my hand out from behind my back and show her the egg-shaped vibrator laying across my palm.

"I've been holding onto this for a while, and I can't think of anyone who would be more deserving of it than my pretty little pet."

Her eyes are still fixed on the vibrator, and her cheeks have flushed a deep shade of pink.

"Oh, I've never used anything like that before, Sir."

She's squirming in the bed, and I can see the way she's clenching her thighs together, letting me know the sight of the toy has caused an ache at her core.

"Don't worry, pet," I say, as I push her legs apart with my empty hand. "This is remote-controlled. So tonight, when you're alone in bed, I'll still be able to play with your needy little cunt and make you come. And in the meantime, you can wear it inside you as a reminder of me."

"O-okay, Sir," she replies, her breathing heavy.

"Good girl," I reply, then I drop the toy onto the bed and grab her knees, tugging her forward until her ass is at the edge of the mattress and her pussy is on display. "Now hold yourself open for me."

She does as I order, and I let out a satisfied growl as I stare down at her glistening slit. Her lips are already swollen and parted, and I can see the wetness gathering at her entrance.

"That's my good girl. Spread yourself so I can have a better look."

I wait a few seconds, watching as the blush on her cheeks deepens, then I lean down and place a gentle kiss on her clit. She lets out a gasp and her hips buck upwards, but I press a hand to her lower stomach and force her back down.

"No moving, pet. Hold yourself open and don't let go."

"Yes, Sir," she whimpers, and I can hear the longing in her voice.

"That's it, good girl," I praise, then I pick up the toy again and bring it up to her pussy.

I press the tip of the vibrator against her soaked entrance, and a small moan falls from her lips as I start to ease it inside her. Her pussy clenches, and her walls grip the toy, but the vibrator is smaller than my cock, and she takes it easily.

Once it's fully seated inside her, I give her a satisfied smile.

"Such a good girl," I say, stroking a finger along her thigh. "Now, you are not allowed to take it out unless you need the bathroom, in which case, you will put it straight back in as soon as you're finished and cleaned up. Do you understand, pet?"

"Yes, Sir," she whimpers, squirming a little as her needy little cunt clenches around the toy.

"Good girl," I say. "Now get your phone for me, Ellie. I need to give you my number so that when your mom is asleep tonight, you can call me and I can hear you as I make you come for me."

She does as I ask, and once her phone is unlocked, she hands it over to me. I enter my number, then send a text to my own phone.

"There, now I have your number too, pet," I say, placing the phone on the bedside table.

I lean down and press a kiss to her lips, then move down to her breasts, laving my tongue over her nipples.

"Alex," she moans, and I can hear the impatience in her voice.

"Do you have something to say, pet?" I ask, raising an eyebrow at her as I move away from her nipples.

"It's just that having the vibrator inside me is making me so needy, Sir. Please, will you make me come one more time before I have to go home?"

I smirk.

"You're a very greedy girl today, pet," I say. "I like that. A lot."

"Please," she repeats, giving me the most adorable pleading look.

I groan. "Fuck, you are irresistible."

I slide a hand down her stomach, teasing my fingertips over her clit. She lets out a soft gasp, and her pussy clenches around the toy inside her.

"Yes," she moans. "Oh, Sir, please."

I stroke her clit, circling the sensitive bud, and her hips arch up, seeking more contact.

"Sir," she breathes, her voice hoarse and needy.

"I've got you, Ellie," I murmur. "Just relax and let me take care of you."

I rub her clit harder, faster, and her breath comes in short gasps as her orgasm builds.

"Oh, Sir, yes," she cries, her body trembling with need.

I lean down and suck her nipple into my mouth, and the extra stimulation sends her over the edge. She lets out a sharp cry, and her body stiffens, her back arching off the bed as she comes.

"That's it, pet," I growl, rubbing her clit through her orgasm. "Come for me."

She shudders and moans, her hips rocking against my hand as she rides out the waves of pleasure.

"Oh, Sir," she moans. "Thank you."

I grin down at her, enjoying the blissful look on her face.

"You're welcome, pet," I say, brushing my lips across her forehead. "When you feel that toy inside you tonight, I want it to be a reminder that I own this pretty little pussy now, and that I control whether or not you are allowed to come, Ellie."

Her eyes go wide and her cheeks flush with color.

"Y-yes, Sir," she stammers, her voice slightly nervous, but the arousal in her eyes is obvious.

"Good girl," I say. "Now, as much as it pains me, I need to get you home."

I give her one last kiss before forcing myself to get out of the bed and gather her clothes.

As she dresses, I can't help but feel a deep sense of satisfaction. She's mine now. My sweet, obedient little pet.

And I'm never going to let her go.

I can't even remember why I was so scared of falling in love. Now it's happened; it's the easiest, most natural thing in the world.

Chapter Ten

Ellie:

The evening seems to drag by, and I find myself having to fight constantly against the urge to check my phone for messages from Alex. God knows how Mom will react if she sees me looking at my phone more than normal. She'd be even more convinced than ever that I've got a boyfriend.

Well, technically I have now, and the heavy weight of the vibrator inside me is a reminder of that, even though it's still switched off. But Mom really doesn't need to know about my new relationship.

She's been quiet ever since I got home from work, although now and then I'll catch her giving me the stink eye. I guess she's still mad at me for walking out on our conversation about Alex last night. It's kind of nice though. When she's quiet like this, it gives me more time to think about my sexy older neighbor.

Every time I think about our afternoon together, I want to smile from ear-to-ear, but that's just another thing I have to keep hidden until I'm alone. God, I really can't wait until I've got a place of my own.

By ten o'clock, Mom has passed out in front of the TV, and judging by the loud snores currently coming from her, I'm guessing she'll be out like a light for a good few hours.

So I grab my phone and creep upstairs, smiling broadly to myself as I see a message from Alex.

Alex: *I can't wait to play with your needy little pussy soon. I'm going to make it purr all night long.*

I nibble on my lower lip as a rush of arousal floods my body. I can't wait either.

With hasty steps, I make my way to my bedroom and shut and lock the door behind me, before dialing Alex's number. He picks up on the second ring.

"Hello, pet," he says, and the deep, rumbling sound of his voice sends a shiver down my spine.

"Hi, Alex," I say, my own voice coming out a little breathy.

"How has your evening been?" he asks. "Has everything been okay with your mom?"

I shrug, even though I know he can't see me. But the fact he seems worried about me is enough to make my heart beat a little faster for him. He's everything I could ever want in a man, and I'm suddenly so grateful that I took a chance and went to visit him at Surrender that first night.

"It's been fine," I tell him. "I've been thinking about you a lot, though."

"Good girl. And are you ready to come for me again, my sweet pet?" he asks.

Before the sentence is even fully out of his mouth, I feel a gentle buzzing sensation between my thighs that sends a warmth radiating outward from my core. The surprise of it makes my knees buckle slightly, and I stumble towards my bed, sitting down on the edge of it.

Little whimpers escape me, and I squeeze my thighs together to increase the sensations created by the toy inside me.

"Yes, Sir," I moan. "I'm so ready."

"Good girl. Are you naked for me, Ellie?"

"N-not yet," I stammer as the vibrations seem to increase slightly, causing a fresh wave of pleasure to wash over me. "I came straight to my room and locked the door."

"Take your clothes off," he orders, his voice low and commanding. "It doesn't matter that I can't see you right now. I still want my pretty plaything to be naked when I'm toying with her wet little cunt."

Oh god, it drives me wild when he talks dirty like that. I quickly stand back up, dropping my phone onto the bed and yanking off my shirt. My jeans and panties quickly follow, leaving me completely bare.

"I'm naked, Sir," I breathe, picking the phone back up. Anticipation is racing through me, fueled by the pleasant sensations emanating from my center.

"Good girl," he praises. "Now lay down on the bed and spread your legs for me. The way you would do if I were there with you and you were displaying yourself to me."

I let out a little whimper, and my pussy clenches around the vibrator as I lay down and spread my legs wide.

"I wish you were here, Sir," I say, unable to hide the longing from my voice.

"Soon, pet. But right now, all I want you to focus on is how good it feels to have me playing with your needy little pussy. Can you do that for me?"

"Yes, Sir."

"Good girl," he growls. "Now, reach between your thighs and tease your clit for me. Imagine it's my fingers stroking and circling your sensitive little bud. Imagine it's my tongue tracing patterns across it, flicking and licking and bringing you closer to the edge."

I do as he says, and I let out a loud moan. The sensations of the vibrator paired with the mental images he's describing are so overwhelming that my body trembles, and I can feel my inner walls fluttering and clenching around the toy.

"That's my good girl," he murmurs. "Let yourself feel the pleasure. Let yourself get close to coming for me. But don't come without permission."

"Yes, Sir," I moan, continuing to tease my clit as the vibrations become stronger and stronger, driving me closer to the edge.

The fact that he desires complete control over my body and my pleasure, even when we're not in the same room, is an intoxicating feeling. His power and confidence are so damn sexy, and that alone would be enough to get my needy pussy desperate for an orgasm.

"Fuck, pet," he growls, his voice thick with lust. "The sounds you're making are so fucking sexy. It's making me rock hard."

My breath hitches, and my hips buck up off the bed, grinding against my hand.

"Are you touching yourself too, Sir?" I ask, imagining him sitting on the couch where he'd spanked me, with his hard cock in his hand.

"I am, pet," he confirms. "And it's all your fault. You and those sexy little moans."

The mental image of him pleasuring himself while talking to me is almost too much. A fresh wave of desire rushes through me, and my thighs shake with the effort of keeping myself from coming.

"Oh god, Alex," I cry. "I'm so close."

"Not yet, Ellie," he says, his voice firm. "Don't come until I tell you to."

"Yes, Sir," I whimper, biting down on my lower lip to hold back the tide of pleasure threatening to overwhelm me.

"I'm so close," he groans. "Stop playing with your clit now, pet. I want full control of your pussy."

I let out a frustrated moan as I use all the willpower I possess to pull my hand away from that aching spot between my thighs. My entire body is trembling with the intense desire coursing through me, and I feel like I'll go crazy if he doesn't let me come soon.

"I need to come, Sir," I whimper, still keeping my voice low in case Mom wakes up. "I'm desperate."

"Then beg for it," he growls, something in his voice sounding almost feral as he gets closer to his own release. "Beg me to let you come."

As he says the words, the vibrations coming from the toy come to an abrupt stop, and I can't hold back the whine that escapes me.

"Please, Sir," I say, not even trying to hide the desperation in my voice. "I need to come. Please let me come for you. I promise to always be a good girl for you. Always obey you. Please, please, please, Sir."

I can hear him breathing heavily on the other end of the phone, and the sound of his pleasure-filled grunts sends another rush of desire through me.

"That's it, pet," he growls, the vibrator between my thighs beginning to hum again. "Beg for it. Beg me to make you come. Show me how much you want it."

The vibrations increase, and they're almost strong enough to send me over the edge. Almost.

"I do want it, Sir," I whine. "So bad. Please, Sir. I'm so close."

"Fuck," he groans. "I'm going to come, pet. Come with me."

He increases the intensity of the vibrations again, and I cry out, my back arching off the bed as pleasure crashes through me.

"Oh god, yes," he grunts, and I can hear the relief in his voice as he reaches his own climax.

For a few moments, all I can hear is his ragged breathing. Then his voice comes through the phone, his tone soft and satisfied.

"You were such a good girl for me, Ellie," he murmurs.

"Thank you, Sir," I say, barely able to string a coherent thought together as I slowly come down from my own release.

"You're welcome, pet."

As we lay there in the afterglow, the sound of each other's breathing and occasional little gasps filling the air, I can't help but wish once more that he was here beside me.

"I miss you, Alex," I say softly, letting my eyelids fall closed as I relax into the softness of the mattress.

"I miss you, too, Ellie. But hopefully not for much longer. I'm going to come see you again tomorrow, okay? I'll find a way for us to get some time together."

"Okay, Sir," I say, yawning loudly.

"Sleep well, my sweet girl," he says, his voice a gentle, soothing rumble in my ear.

"You, too, Alex."

We hang up, and I snuggle down beneath the blankets, letting the exhaustion that's been building over the past few days take over.

I drift off with a smile on my face, the heavy weight of the vibrator between my thighs a reminder that Alex has got me.

No matter what.

And that makes me feel safer than ever.

Chapter Eleven

Alex:

"What's got you so distracted today?" Charlie asks as we sit together in his office.

We're co-owners of Surrender, and lifelong friends. He found his submissive, Amelia, just a few months ago, and he's been sickeningly happy ever since.

It's almost lunchtime, and I've been helping him for the last hour put together some legal documents for his business, but I can't stop thinking about seeing Ellie soon. I'd text her this morning to tell her I'd be picking her up from the library at twelve to take her out for lunch, and I'd got a quick reply confirming she'd be there waiting for me. Complete with a little heart emoji at the end of her message.

She's so cute, and her enthusiasm is infectious.

"Earth to Alex!" Charlie's voice cuts through my thoughts, and I turn to look at him.

"What?" I ask.

"I asked what's got you so distracted, man," he says, leaning back in his chair and looking at me with curiosity in his eyes.

I consider lying and saying it's just work. But I don't want to lie to him. We've known each other long enough that he can tell when I'm bullshitting him, anyway.

"There's this girl," I admit, shrugging like it's no big deal.

A smirk pulls at his lips. "The pretty brunette who appeared at the club the other night? The new girl?"

"Yeah," I sigh, running a hand through my hair. "Except she's not new to me. She's my neighbor."

"What?!"

I give him a rundown of what's been happening between Ellie and me, including filling him in about the problems with her mom, and when I finish, Charlie is grinning at me.

"It sounds like you've got it bad, man."

I laugh and nod. "Yeah. So bad that I've been looking at new houses all morning before our meeting. I want to get her away from her mom, but moving Ellie in with me won't cut it. Not when the issue will still be right next door."

"Have you told her about this?"

I shake my head. "Not yet. I want it to be a surprise. I've already found a couple of places with potential and set up viewings. Once I've got something lined up, I'll tell her then. I don't want to get her hopes up if nothing comes from it."

"Makes sense," he says, nodding in agreement. "I hope something works out. She deserves some peace. And she sounds like a really sweet girl."

"She is." I pause and sigh again. "I'm crazy about her, man. I know it's early, and we haven't been together for very long, but... I just feel like she's meant to be mine."

"That's how it was with Amelia and me," he admits, a wistful look in his eyes. "Once I knew she was the one for me, there was no denying it. I had to have her."

"Ellie is the same," I tell him. "Just knowing she's next door, so close, but just out of reach, it's driving me fucking crazy. She's all I think about."

"When are you going to see her again?"

"After our meeting. I'm picking her up from work and taking her to lunch."

"At least you haven't got long to wait then," he says.

A shrill ringtone cuts through the air, and I glance down at my phone.

"It's my mom," I say. "Mind if I take it?"

"Go ahead. I think we're done here, anyway."

I press the button to answer the call. "Hey, Mom. What's up?"

"Hi, sweetie. How have you been?"

Hearing her voice makes me smile. My busy schedule usually stops me from seeing her as often as I'd like, but I've always been close to my mom.

"I've been good thanks, just snowed under with work like usual."

I consider telling her about Ellie, but it's still early days, and I don't want to get Mom's hopes up just yet. She's pretty much given up on the idea of me ever finding love.

"You're always working," she admonishes.

"I know. It's worth it though. What's up, Mom?"

"Well, I'm sitting here with your Dad, Alex. We've been chatting all morning, clearing the air about everything that happened in the past. And he says he'd like to apologize to you, too."

"Oh," I say, staring into the corner of my office for a long moment.

I haven't seen Dad since he divorced Mom when I was nine years old. And even though I thought I'd never want to see him again, I can't deny that I'm curious about him. He is my father, after all, even if he did abandon his family.

Maybe seeing him and hearing his apology will be the closure I need so I can finally put my past behind me and settle down peacefully with Ellie.

"When is he free to meet up?" I ask, surprised at how choked I sound.

"Hold on a second," Mom says, then I hear her talking quietly to someone in the background.

My ears strain to pick up the deep voice of the man she's talking to, feeling tears prick my eyes as I realize I can't even properly remember what my own father's voice sounds like. I quickly swipe the tears away, but not before Charlie gives me a curious look.

"He said he can meet up any time today," Mom says when she comes back to the phone.

"Okay, well, I have a lunch appointment soon, but I can meet him at one when it's finished."

For some reason, now I know Dad is back in the picture, I feel an urgency to see him. I want to find out why he did what he did, so that I can make sure I never end up like him. It seems important now I've met the woman I want to spend my life with.

I hear muffled voices on the other end of the line once more, but Mom is back in a few seconds.

"He said that's fine," she says. "Where do you want to meet him?"

I give her the name of the coffee shop where I'll be taking Ellie for lunch, and we say our goodbyes.

"What was all that about?" Charlie asks. "Are you okay?"

"My dad's in town," I say, a strange, choked laugh coming out.

"Wait, what?!"

I shake my head, feeling slightly numb. "I know. It's weird, right?"

"So what's going on?"

"Mom and Dad have apparently been talking all morning. I guess he wants to apologize and try to fix things between us."

Charlie is watching me with a careful, assessing gaze. "And you're going to meet up with him?"

"Yeah," I say, rubbing the back of my neck. "I can't deny that I'm curious about the guy. Even if he did abandon us all those years ago."

"Well, good luck with it, man," Charlie says. "You've got my number. Let me know if you need anything. This is huge, and I'm here for you if you need me."

"Thanks," I say, smiling gratefully at him. "I'd better go. Ellie will be waiting for me."

"You can't keep the little minx waiting," he agrees, flashing me a wicked grin.

I laugh and nod. "See you later."

I stand and walk out of Charlie's office, my briefcase in one hand and a thousand thoughts swirling around in my head.

It's been such a long time since I saw my dad. And now that I'm actually going to see him, it feels surreal. I can only hope that whatever happens, it will be for the best.

For all of us.

Especially for Ellie. I want to be a much better husband and father than my dad ever was.

Ellie deserves the world, and I want to be the one to give it to her.

Chapter Twelve

Ellie:

"Isn't it a little soon for me to be meeting your parents?" I ask Alex, a teasing grin pulling at my lips.

He laughs and reaches across the table, taking my hand in his. The affectionate touch sends little tingles shooting through my body. A week ago, I felt as though I wasn't really on his radar, besides polite conversations in the front yard whenever our schedules lined up as we were coming and going. But now, I'm having lunch with him, and he's treating me like a girlfriend in public.

I just wish he'd given me a little more notice that I might be meeting his father today.

"It's not like that," he says, chuckling softly as he pulls my hand towards him and begins pressing little kisses against the knuckles. "I haven't seen him since I was a kid, and he called up out of the blue this morning wanting to meet. I just wanted to get it over with as quickly as possible. Besides, I asked him to meet me here at one, and I'm guessing you'll already be back at the library by then, right?"

I sit up a little straighter in my chair as I listen to him. "Oh wow, I knew your parents got divorced, but I didn't realise you hadn't seen him in that long. So this is a pretty big deal, huh? How are you feeling?"

He gives me a small smile and shrugs his shoulders. "A little nervous, I guess. I don't really know what to expect. Mom said they've been talking all morning, and he seems really apologetic about everything that had happened in the past. I think he wants to apologise to me, too."

"I hope it all goes okay," I say, feeling a surge of protectiveness for the man sitting across the table from me.

"Thanks," he says. "I'm sure it will be fine. Now, get over here, Ellie. You're too far away for my liking."

I can't help but giggle as he tugs on my hand and pulls me towards him, guiding me to sit in his lap. "Should we be sitting like this in public?"

Alex chuckles and dips his head, his lips brushing against my ear as he speaks. "I don't care where we are, pet," he says in that deep, husky voice that never fails to create a flutter deep in the pit of my stomach. "I always want you as close as possible. Besides, it's not like we're doing anything inappropriate. Now, if I were doing some of the other things I've been thinking about the entire time we've been eating lunch, then I could see why you'd be worried."

He nips gently at my earlobe, and a growl rumbles upwards from somewhere deep in his chest. His suggestive words force a gasp from my lips, and I begin fidgeting as a heat builds between my thighs.

"Careful, pet," he groans, still keeping his voice low so others around us won't hear. "If you keep wriggling in my lap like that, I'll have no choice but to bend you over this table and turn your ass a pretty shade of pink. Then maybe I'd pull those sexy little panties off of you and fuck you hard, right here. Would you like that, Ellie?"

"Sir," I whimper, unsure if I want him to stop saying such filthy things in the middle of a coffee shop, or if I want to hear more and more of the dirty ideas in his head.

A heat creeps up my face, turning my cheeks a bright shade of red, and the heat between my thighs intensifies until it feels like an inferno. I know he would never go through with doing anything like that here. For a start, we'd get arrested for public indecency. But the knowledge that a man as sexy, intelligent and successful as Alex wants me in that way is an intoxicating feeling I'm not sure I'll ever get used to.

"Mmm, I love the way you say that," he purrs, his breath warm on my skin.

I can feel the hard length of his erection pressing against me through his suit pants, and I squirm some more. He responds by biting down on my earlobe and sliding his hands around to grip my hips tightly, stopping me from moving.

"Enough, pet," he growls, his voice a warning. "Otherwise I won't be able to control myself any longer."

I whine softly and lean back into him, enjoying the feeling of his strong, muscular arms wrapped around me. "I'm sorry, Sir," I whisper.

We stay like that, cuddled together, until Alex glances at the time on his watch.

"Time for you to get back to work, my sweet pet," he murmurs.

Reluctantly, I pull myself away from him and stand. "I just need to go to the bathroom first," I say, then glance around the coffee shop, looking for the sign that points towards the restrooms.

I see a sign for the ladies' room on the far side of the room and begin making my way over. As I glance back over my shoulder, I find Alex watching me, his dark eyes smouldering with lust. I have to turn back quickly, though, because the look he's giving me makes me feel like a piece of meat. A tasty meal that he's planning to devour later on.

It's not a bad feeling at all, and a small smile plays on my lips as I hurry towards the restrooms, eager to get back out to him.

Once I'm done, I wash my hands and check my reflection in the mirror. My cheeks are flushed, and my pupils are wide, but I don't look too bad otherwise.

I push open the door and step out into the hallway. I'm just turning the corner that leads back into the main area of the coffee shop when I catch sight of a tall, dark-haired man entering the building.

I stop in my tracks, my heart hammering hard inside my chest. Shit. What the fuck is Mark doing here? I haven't seen him since I was fifteen, since the night he and my Mom had a huge screaming match and she told him never to come back.

As I watch him saunter across the coffee shop as if he hasn't got a care in the world, I can't help but hate him. He always was a cocky bastard, and it doesn't look as if that's changed. I think it's that unwavering confidence that meant he was always such a success with women, too. Mom included.

I press myself against the wall and pray that he doesn't spot me, but his attention seems fixed firmly elsewhere. On Alex.

Mark walks over to the table where I'd just been sitting and, for a moment, Alex doesn't see him as he's looking down at something on his phone. But as soon as Alex glances up and sees who's standing there, his expression turns to one of surprise.

Mark says something, his arms open as if he expects a hug, but Alex's face hardens slightly and he gives a small shake of his head. My heart drops down into my stomach as the man who ruined my mom's life, and mine by extension, sits down in the place I'd been sitting while eating.

Oh god. He's Alex's father.

I feel as though I've been punched in the gut as I stare, unable to look away from the two men sitting opposite each other just a few yards away.

Alex's father is the reason my own mother spiralled into a depression so deep I couldn't reach her. My mind flashes back to memories from my teenage years. Mom was drunk, the house was a mess, and I spent all my time trying to take care of both of us so that the authorities wouldn't take me away from her.

My throat feels tight, and tears burn behind my eyes. I can't believe Alex's father is the same man who destroyed my family, the same man I've hated for so many years.

I slip back into the restroom, hiding myself from the scene playing out before me, and slide down the wall until my butt hits the floor. The tears that have been threatening to spill over finally fall, and I bury my face in my hands, sobbing.

How could the man I've fallen in love with be related to that piece of shit? How am I supposed to be able to trust Alex now that I know what his father is capable of doing to women?

I just don't know if I can.

Chapter Thirteen

Alex:

"It's so good to see you, son," says the man sitting across from me, and I can't help but wince inwardly.

It feels strange seeing my father again after almost four decades, and hearing him call me son leaves a sour taste in my mouth. He may have helped to create me, but he's no father to me. Not anymore.

He doesn't look the same as I remember him looking all those years ago. The hair that had once been so dark is now speckled with a generous amount of gray, and there are deep lines around his mouth and eyes that weren't there when I last saw him. He looks like a tired old man.

"What are you doing here, Dad?"

"I just wanted to reconnect, son. And apologize for everything that happened."

"My name is Alex," I say, the words coming out a little more brusquely than I intend them to be. "I'd appreciate it if you could use it."

He shifts awkwardly in his chair and gives a little nod. "Of course, Alex. So I just want you to know that I'm sorry for being such a bad father to you, and a bad husband to your mom. I was just young and stupid, and I made a lot of mistakes. And I regret every single one of them."

I just continue watching him. Somehow, all the anticipation and excitement about meeting him have disappeared, and all I can think about was how he abandoned me and my mom. I guess I'd been hoping he would have a good reason, and in my eyes, being young and dumb isn't enough.

When I don't say anything, Dad continues talking. "I've missed you over the years, and I've thought about you every single day."

"Then why didn't you get in touch before?" I ask, unable to hide the bitterness from my voice.

Images of all the events he missed flash through my mind. The birthdays and Christmases. My graduation. Every single time, there had been something, or should I say someone, important missing from the proceedings, making me feel like my own father didn't give a shit about me.

"I didn't want to disrupt your life," he says, his face contorting with guilt. "I'd already done enough of that. And then, as you grew up and became a man, I didn't think you'd want me turning up and ruining everything. So I figured it was best to leave you alone and let you live your life."

"That's not what a father does," I say, my jaw clenched tight.

"I know," he says. "And if I could go back and change things, I would."

"But you can't," I point out. "And the damage is already done."

"I know," he repeats. "And that's why I want to apologize. So I could let you know how much I regret my actions. And maybe even try to build some sort of relationship with you."

He stares at me, and for a moment, I see a flicker of pain and regret in his eyes. It's almost enough to make me think about forgiving him. Almost.

"Well, thank you for apologizing," I say. "That means a lot. But I'm not sure it changes anything."

Dad lets out a sigh, and my gaze drifts in the direction of the restrooms. Why hasn't Ellie come out yet? She's going to be late back to work. Worry starts to claw at my chest. But then Dad starts talking again, pulling my attention back to him.

"I got married again thirty years ago," he says, smiling happily as he pulls out his phone. "And I've got two sons, who are twenty-four and twenty-six. You've got two half-brothers, Alex, if you'd ever like to meet them one day."

He scrolls through some images on his phone and pulls up a picture of two young men. They both look more like Dad than I do, and jealousy surges through me. They got to know what it was like to grow up with a father, but I didn't.

"Congratulations," I say, trying to force a smile.

"Thanks," he says, missing the obvious discomfort I feel.

I have no idea why I thought this would be a good idea. He hasn't even given me a real reason why he left us. This is all just bullshit. I've wasted enough time already, and I want this meeting to be over with.

"Listen," I say, glancing over towards the restrooms once more. "I'm sorry, but I have to get going. I've got a very important business meeting soon, and I can't be late. Thank you for coming and talking to me."

"Yeah, no worries," he says, a hint of sadness creeping into his voice.

As I stand, Ellie emerges from the hallway that leads to the bathrooms. My eyes widen as I take in her appearance. Her hair is disheveled, while her face is red and streaked with tears. As she stalks over to us, her hands are clenched into fists at her side. I've never seen her like this, and for a moment, I'm shocked into silence.

She doesn't stop walking until she's standing right next to the table, and the look on her face is enough to make a lump form in my throat. Her gaze is fixed on Dad, and there's so much hatred burning in her eyes that it makes my heart twist in pain.

"You fucking asshole!" she hisses through gritted teeth. "You've got some nerve coming back to this town after everything you did."

My dad jumps up from his seat, a shocked look on his face. "Ellie, well, this is a surprise."

I blink, watching the scene unfold in front of me with utter confusion.

"What's going on?" I ask, taking a step closer to Ellie.

Mark might be my father, but it's Ellie who deserves my loyalty right now. Especially when she's clearly upset about something.

"I can't believe you had the audacity to show your face in this town," Ellie snaps, completely ignoring me. "Do you have any idea how much pain you caused my family?"

"Keep your voice down, Ellie," he says, glancing nervously around the coffee shop.

My mind reels, slowly slotting all the puzzle pieces together in my head until I think I know what's going on. There's only one man Ellie would be this mad at, and that's the married man who led her mother on for several years when she was younger.

The man who is also my father.

"I can't believe it," I mutter, feeling the rage rising up inside me until it threatens to choke me. "You haven't changed at all, have you, Dad? You come here telling me you're happily married and that you're a great father to your kids, when in reality, you were still fucking around a decade ago, and you probably still are now."

Dad's face turns white, and his mouth opens and closes repeatedly as he tries to find something to say.

"I'm done with you," I spit out. "And if you have any respect for me at all, you won't come anywhere near me, my mom, or Ellie again."

"Please, Alex," Dad pleads. "I can explain."

"Explain what? That you're a piece of shit who can't keep his dick in his pants for more than five fucking seconds?"

"Alex," he says, reaching out and grabbing hold of my arm.

Without even thinking about what I'm doing, I grab his hand and shove it off me, sending him sprawling backwards and crashing to the floor. We've got the attention of everyone in the coffee shop, and I can feel multiple sets of eyes on me as I turn to Ellie, forgetting about the pathetic excuse of a man currently pulling himself up from the floor.

"Ellie, are you okay?" I ask, my voice softer now.

As I reach out to pull her into my arms, she steps out of my reach.

"I can't do this right now," she says, holding back tears. "I... I just need some time to think, okay? This is... it's just too much. I'm sorry, Alex. I just... I need to go."

She turns and flees from the coffee shop, leaving me standing alone and watching her leave.

"I'm so sorry," says Dad, who's finally standing on his own two feet again.

But I ignore him and grab my jacket, racing out to follow Ellie.

She's the only thing that matters to me right now, and I'm determined to prove to her I'm nothing like my father.

Chapter Fourteen

Ellie:

I hurry away from the coffee shop, unable to think straight. Tears blur my vision, and my throat feels so tight it's almost hard to breathe.

All those years of hating Mark. All those years of wishing he'd never met my mother. And now I find out the man who broke my mother's heart is Alex's father. The one person I'd begun to care about more than anyone else in the world.

Am I going to end up being as hurt by love as my mom was? Maybe she was right all along and men just aren't worth the hassle.

I'm so lost in my thoughts that I don't even hear Alex calling my name, or the sound of his footsteps getting closer.

"Ellie, wait," he says, grabbing hold of my arm and pulling me to a halt.

He moves in front of me, and I'm forced to look into his eyes, which are filled with so much concern, it makes my chest ache.

"Ellie, please don't push me away. I know you're hurting right now, but you don't have to deal with this on your own. You have me, and I promise you I'll never hurt you like that bastard hurt your mother."

He pulls me into an alleyway between two stores, away from the prying eyes of people passing us on the sidewalk, and I let him back me up against the wall. With gentle fingertips, he brushes the tears off my cheeks while I try to take some deep breaths.

"My dad died when I was six," I say when I feel a little calmer. "It felt like my mom was sad for my entire childhood. And I can still remember the day she met Mark when I was twelve. It was like she became a different person overnight. She was happy. She used to smile again, and I'd catch her singing whenever she was getting ready to go out on a date with him. I finally thought life was going to get a little better, you know?"

Alex nods quietly, reaching up to stroke his fingers through my hair. The gentle touch makes something inside me melt a little, and I want to step closer to him and snuggle in against his warmth and his strength. I've always felt safe in his arms, and I hate Mark a little more now for putting this doubt about Alex in my mind.

"And then all of a sudden, my happy mom was gone again. Only this time, she was even more upset than I remember her being when Dad died. Maybe because Dad had never chosen to leave her. It was out of his control. But Mark had chosen to betray her. He'd knowingly betrayed her every day for three years, and it broke her, Alex."

My voice cracks on a sob, and Alex pulls me in against his chest, wrapping his arms around me.

"I'm so sorry," he whispers. "I promise you that's not the kind of man I am. I'll never betray you, Ellie. I'm not going to leave you, and I'm not going to break your heart. If you just give me a chance, I'll prove to you how much I love you."

I pull back just enough that I can look up into his eyes, which are shining with unshed tears.

"But how can I know for sure you won't hurt me?" I ask in a pitifully small voice.

Alex sighs and presses a gentle kiss to my forehead. "I guess there are never any guarantees in life, Ellie. But I do know you are the only woman I can see in my future. You're the only one who's ever been able to make me truly happy. And the thought of living the rest of my life without you scares the shit out of me. I've never felt anything like that before. Not even once."

I blink up at him, trying to process the words even though my brain already feels so damn overwhelmed by everything that's happened today. I so want to believe him. There's a part of me that is desperate to accept his words and allow myself to love him completely.

But there is another part of me that's so fucking afraid of ending up like my mom.

"I met up with Dad today for one reason only," he continues. "I've spent my entire life avoiding relationships because of everything I saw happening between my mom and dad when I was growing up. If I'm honest, I was worried I'd be like him. That I'd just hurt any woman who loved me. So I kept everyone at arm's length. I hoped that if I met up with him today and heard why he did the things he did, then maybe I could put my own lifetime of fears behind me. So that then I'd be ready to be a much better husband to you and a better father to our kids than he ever was."

Alex looks down at me, tucking a stray lock of hair behind my ear. My throat starts to burn, and I realize I'm holding my breath, waiting for whatever else he has to say. He's already thinking about things like that? About us getting married and having children?

"But when I met him today, he couldn't seem to give me a real reason. He's just a prick, Ellie, who puts himself and his own selfish needs before everyone else. And I might not be perfect, but I know I'm not like him. I could never fool around with anyone else now that I've found you. Do you want to know how I know that, pet?"

My breath hitches, and I nod my head, unable to tear my gaze away from his face. It's like I'm mesmerized by everything he's saying, and bit by bit, I can feel all the tension and fear melting away.

"Because I'm fucking obsessed with you, Ellie. Ever since that first night together, I haven't been able to stop thinking about you. You're my first thought when I wake up in the morning and my last thought before I fall asleep. And when you're not with me, it feels like there's a big fucking part of me missing. I love you, Ellie, and I want a future with you. I want us to grow old together and have lots of kids. I have never, ever felt that before. You're the only person I can imagine my life with."

"Oh, Alex," I whisper, blinking away the tears.

"I've even spent this morning looking for a new house for us, so we can move away from your mom and we won't have to hide our relationship. I'm serious about us, Ellie. Fuck, you'd be living with me already if I had my way, but I know your mom wouldn't leave us alone if we were just living next door to her."

My mind spins with each new word from his lips. I try to find something to say, but I'm too overwhelmed to think straight.

Instead, I lean into him, needing to feel his lips on mine. He doesn't hesitate, pressing his mouth to mine, and all the emotions of the moment crashes over me like a wave. As we kiss, Alex pulls me closer and tangles his hands in my hair. Every single part of my body is screaming for him, and I wrap my arms around his neck, trying to get even closer to him.

He pulls away slightly, resting his forehead against mine.

"I don't want to lose you," he murmurs. "But if you need some space or some time to think, then that's okay. You just tell me what you need."

"I don't need space," I tell him, and it feels like a weight has been lifted from my chest. "I need you, Alex."

"Oh, thank fuck," he mutters, and he captures my mouth in a fierce kiss.

His hands slide down my back, and then he grabs my ass and hoists me up, forcing me to wrap my legs around his waist. He presses me against the wall, his hips grinding into mine as he kisses me with so much passion and intensity, it leaves me gasping for breath.

"I fucking love you," he groans. "I swear I'm going to make you happy, Ellie."

"You already do," I gasp, rolling my hips against him. "And Alex, I love you too."

He smiles down at me, happiness shining in his eyes.

"You really mean that?"

I nod and reach up to touch his cheek, letting my fingers trace the curve of his jaw.

"I really do."

Alex kisses me again, and the world around us disappears. Right now, it's just me and him and the feeling of pure happiness washing over me. I want to freeze this moment in time and live in it forever.

We are going to be okay.

He pulls back a little and looks down at me, a wicked grin on his lips. "Unless you want me to fuck you here where anybody might see us, we should probably go somewhere more private. I intend to spend the rest of the day showing you just how crazy I am about you, pet."

"Okay, Sir," I whisper, feeling a giddy excitement building inside me. "Let's go."

Alex puts me down and takes hold of my hand, leading me out of the alleyway and towards his car. As we walk, he wraps his arm around my shoulders and holds me close, and I lean into his side, loving the way he's touching me in public without caring who sees.

And for the first time in a very long time, everything feels right.

Chapter Fifteen

Alex:

As we pull into my garage, Ellie is crouching down in the front seat so her mom won't see her if she happens to look out the window at just the right moment. God, I can't wait for us to move out, so we don't have to sneak around like this. I want to be able to show her off proudly and let everyone in the world know that she's mine.

I press the button on the remote that closes the door, and Ellie pops up again, a sheepish smile on her face. She called her boss on the drive home to let them know that she needed to take the afternoon off work because of a family emergency. I know she's worried that if she keeps calling in sick that she'll lose her job, but I'll take good care of her if that happens. In my dreams of the future, she'll be a mom to lots of little ones, so she might not even want to work when that happens, anyway. With my income, she certainly doesn't need to.

We both get out of the car, and I rush around to her, pressing her back against the cool metal of the passenger door with my body. She lets out a low moan and looks up at me with heavy-lidded eyes.

"I can't wait until we have our own place, Sir," she says. "Then we won't have to hide anymore."

"I know, pet," I growl. "I feel the same. And don't worry, I'm going to make it happen as fast as I can, Ellie. We'll be in our own house and you'll be wearing my ring and carrying my babies in no time."

I'm already unbuttoning her blouse, ripping it off her body with frantic movements. My dick is rock hard, desperate to be inside her so I can reclaim her as mine after all the stress of today. And it seems she's just as eager. Ellie isn't even bothering with my shirt as she focuses on unzipping my pants and pulling them down enough that she can free my cock.

"Don't you think it's a little too soon to be thinking of babies?" she asks, although I'm surprised she can form a sentence at all with the way she's staring at my dick as if she's mesmerized by the sight of it.

She crouches down, her back still against the car, and runs her tongue along the hard length of my shaft. A low hiss escapes from between my gritted teeth, and my cock jerks in response to the touch.

"Not too soon at all," I growl out, enjoying each exploratory flick of her tongue against my hardened flesh. "After all, we've already had unprotected sex once, and I plan on fucking you raw every time until your stomach is round with my baby."

Her eyes dart up to meet mine, and I can't read the expression in them. Is she turned on or scared? Or a little of both?

"I like the idea of putting my baby in your belly, pet," I add, and she whimpers quietly, her hand reaching up to fondle my balls. "I can't wait to see your body change and your breasts swell as your body makes milk for our child. You're going to be so beautiful, Ellie. And knowing you're carrying my baby will only make you even hotter."

"Oh god," she moans. "What if I'm already pregnant, Alex? I didn't even think about protection last time."

I grin down at her. "If you're already pregnant, then I'll be the happiest man in the whole fucking world, Ellie." Reaching down, I grab her arm gently and pull her up to her feet again. "But that's not going to stop me filling you with more of my seed until I know my baby is definitely growing in your womb."

Her eyes darken, and she nods silently, her chest heaving as her breathing quickens.

"And I'm going to start right now, pet."

I let out a feral growl as I pick her up off the floor and push her back against the side of the car, my hips between her parted thighs. I'm not sure I can even wait until we are inside the main part of the house to claim her. With deft movements, I pull her skirt up and go to pull her panties to the side, only to be met with the soft, wet flesh of her bare pussy lips against my fingertips.

"No panties today?" I grunt as I line the head of my cock up with her slick entrance and pull her down onto my shaft, impaling her with one thrust. Her velvety soft inner walls clamp down around me, and it's so damn good it almost makes me forget my train of thought. "I think my needy little pet was hoping she'd get fucked on her lunch break."

Ellie whimpers and arches her back as she adjusts to my girth.

"Maybe, Sir," she whispers, wrapping her arms around my neck.

I chuckle, enjoying the way her body is clinging to mine. I'm still deep inside her, and her inner muscles are twitching and spasming, like her pussy can't bear the thought of being empty again.

"I know, pet," I groan, starting to thrust slowly in and out. "Your greedy cunt wants my cum so badly, doesn't it?"

"Yes, Sir," she moans, her eyes glazing over with lust. "Please fill me up, Alex."

I growl at her words, picking up my pace and driving my hips up harder, plunging my cock into her.

"You are mine, Ellie," I say, punctuating the words with rough thrusts. "My girlfriend. My future wife. The mother of my future children. I don't care what anyone else thinks about our age gap, or our relationship. You are mine."

"Yours, Sir," she chants breathlessly, her legs tightening around my waist.

Her fingernails dig into my back, and I know she's going to leave scratch marks that will sting later. But I don't give a shit. All that matters right now is that I'm fucking her, claiming her. Reminding her exactly who she belongs to.

I lean in and capture her mouth, kissing her hard and possessively. Ellie whimpers into the kiss, her body trembling with desire as I fuck her roughly. There's something feral inside me, desperate to prove that I'm nothing like my father. To prove that I'm fucking obsessed with her and only her. To prove that she's mine, and I'm hers, and the two of us are meant to be together.

Her moans grow louder, and I know she's close to the edge. So am I. With one last savage thrust, I come hard, shooting my load deep inside her and roaring with pleasure. Her pussy clamps down around me, her body shuddering and her back arching as her own climax rushes over her.

We cling to each other as we both ride out the aftershocks of our orgasms, gasping for breath and shaking. I can't believe how perfect it is, being with her like this. It feels like we were made for each other, and I'll never get enough of her.

"You are perfect, Ellie," I whisper into her ear. "So perfect for me."

"I love you, Alex," she murmurs back, her eyes bright with emotion.

I give her a soft, lingering kiss before slowly sliding out of her and placing her on the ground. She leans against the car and smiles up at me, looking dazed and thoroughly satisfied. I grin down at her, feeling so fucking lucky that I get to spend the rest of my life with this woman.

"Come on," I say, tucking myself back into my pants and zipping them up. "Let's go take a bath together, and then we can see about another round. I was serious when I said I want my baby inside you as quickly as possible."

Ellie's cheeks flush, and her eyes darken with desire again. She licks her lips and nods.

"I want that too, Alex," she says, her voice soft and low. "More than anything."

"Good. And when you go back home later, I'm going to be spending the evening looking at houses again. As soon as I find the perfect one, we'll move out and start our lives together properly."

"Thank you, Sir," she says. "That's all I've ever wanted."

She reaches out and takes my hand, and the two of us walk through to the main part of the house. We might have had a bit of a rocky start, but I'm determined to spend the rest of my life making her happy.

Because Ellie is my entire world, and I'm never letting her go.

Epilogue

Ellie:

It's been six months since that night when I first walked into Surrender and asked Alex to teach me about BDSM. Since then, so much has changed, and I'm nervous about entering the club. While I've visited it plenty of times in the last few months, it's always been to see Alex while it's been closed to the public. But he's determined to show me off at the club he owns, and tonight is the night.

"Relax, pet," Alex whispers into my ear, and his deep, smooth voice sends a shiver of pleasure through my body. "Everything is going to be fine. You look amazing, and everyone is going to love you as much as I do. Well, maybe not quite that much."

He flashes me a lop-sided grin that makes my heart do a flip inside my chest. God, it should be illegal for a man to be this sexy.

"I think you're just biased," I say, giving him a teasing grin of my own in return. "Nobody else is going to think I look great when I look like I'm smuggling in a watermelon under my dress."

I giggle and place a hand on my swollen stomach, feeling the little flutters of movement coming from within. At nearly six months pregnant, there's no disguising the fact that I'm expecting. If Alex didn't get me pregnant during our very first time together, it must have happened pretty quickly after. But perhaps that isn't surprising, considering how determined he was to get me knocked up. I'm fairly certain I was permanently walking funny during the first few weeks of our relationship.

Not that Alex's desires grew any less insatiable after that time. I think my body just got used to his constant attention.

I'm not complaining, though. Alex is one hell of a man, and I can never seem to get enough of him.

He reaches out and places a hand over mine on my stomach, while a dark hunger flashes through his eyes. "I've never seen you look as beautiful or sexy as you do when you're carrying my baby, and trust me when I say that's quite an achievement, because you looked fucking stunning when you first visited this place."

"Charmer," I reply, a slight blush on my cheeks.

Alex grins and shrugs. "I'm just telling the truth. But come on. Let's go inside."

He grips my hand and pulls it away from my bump, before guiding me towards the club. The door man opens the door for us as soon as he sees Alex approaching, and he dips his head in greeting to both of us.

We walk into the club and make our way through the crowds. Everyone we pass says hello to Alex and congratulates us on the pregnancy. I guess the news has been spreading fast among his friends. Alex introduces me to everyone who stops to talk to us, and I'm surprised at how many people seem to know who I am.

When we finally reach the table at the back where his best friends are sitting with their wives and girlfriends, I let out a relieved sigh. I know these people. I met them all at our wedding, and they are regular visitors to the home we now share. They're the family we've built for ourselves, and they are people I feel completely comfortable with.

Even my own mother is slowly starting to warm up to Alex, although I never told her that he's Mark's son. If she knew that, she'd never trust him. At the moment, I'm happy with the fact that she's stopped calling me every day, telling me to leave him. I think the knowledge that she's going to be a grandmother very soon is helping her to handle it all a little better than she might have done otherwise.

"There you are," Elijah says. "We were starting to think you weren't coming."

He's sitting in a chair with Selena, his wife and submissive, sitting in his lap. Her face lights up as she spots me, and she grabs my free hand and tugs me down into the empty seat beside theirs.

"How are you feeling, Ellie?" she asks.

"Don't mind her enthusiasm," Elijah says with a chuckle. "She's missing being pregnant and trying to live vicariously through you right now. But don't worry, I'm doing everything I can to get her knocked up again."

He winks at me before dipping his head to press little kisses against the side of Selena's neck. Her face turns a deep shade of red, but judging by the wide grin she's wearing, she doesn't mind his confession.

I laugh. "I'm feeling good, although this little one is always so active."

Selena nods and grins. "Yeah, just wait until they become a toddler, then you'll understand the real meaning of active. I'm exhausted."

"But not so exhausted that you aren't busy trying for baby number two," Grace teases from across the other side of the table.

Grace is settled in Oliver's lap, and she's looking even more pregnant than I am.

"Wow," I say, taking in the size of her bump. "When are you due? You look like you're about to pop any day now!"

A nervous look flutters across Grace's face, while Oliver smiles at me from ear to ear. "The due date is next week, so it literally could be any day now."

"Don't remind me," Grace groans, covering her face with her hands.

"Actually," Charlie says, clearing his throat. "While the conversation is on babies, Amelia and I have an announcement."

Before they can even say what it is, the entire table erupts into cheers and offers of congratulations. I know they already have a baby at home who is only a few months old, but it seems they didn't want to wait long before they started trying again.

While everyone else is surrounding Charlie and Amelia, Alex crouches beside my chair and whispers in my ear.

"That's what I'm going to be like with you, pet. Eager to breed you as soon as possible after this little one is born."

He places a hand on my stomach and glides it up high enough that his fingertips brush the underside of my breast. A small gasp escapes me, and I glance around the table to see if anyone else saw it, but they are too occupied by Amelia's news to take notice of what we are doing.

"Don't you think we should focus on getting this one out of me before you start planning to put another one in there?" I ask, a teasing grin on my lips.

He chuckles. "Probably. But can you blame me for wanting a big family with you, Ellie? Especially when you look so fucking sexy with your belly swollen with my baby."

He presses a gentle kiss against my cheek, and I shiver as his stubble grazes the delicate skin.

"I love you, Alex," I murmur. "And I want to have lots of babies with you."

"That's my girl," he replies, and a possessive growl rumbles through his chest.

I lean against him, content and happy.

We've come a long way in a short time, and I wouldn't change any of it. Because Alex is perfect for me, and I'm the luckiest woman in the whole world to have him as my Dom, my husband, and the father of my children.

About The Author

Leah Addison and Willow Watkins are the two ~~personalities~~ pen names of one British author who has been obsessed with reading romances ever since she was a teenager. This love of reading has blossomed into an addiction to crafting her own love stories. Very spicy love stories, of course. Things always taste better with a bit of spice added, don't you think?

If you'd like to stalk her online, check out the following link: **https://allmylinks.com/willow-watkins**

Milton Keynes UK
Ingram Content Group UK Ltd.
UKHW032317121024
449481UK00012B/443